# e-Ternity

A Novel

*Jeff Carreira*

e-Ternity
By Jeff Carreira

Copyright © 2020 Jeff Carreira
Published by Transdimensional Fiction
An Imprint of Emergence Education Press

ISBN-13: 978-1-7357886-0-9

Transdimensional Fiction
P.O. Box 63767
Philadelphia, PA 19147

www.transdimensionalfiction.com

Cover design by Silvia Rodrigues

# e-Ternity

*A Novel*

JEFF CARREIRA

*There is no route out of the maze.*
*The maze shifts as you move through it,*
*because it is alive.*

— Philip K. Dick

# CHAPTER ONE

What is it that I want to tell you? What do I want to share? It has something to do with becoming unstuck from reality. It is similar to how Billy Pilgrim was unstuck from time in the novel *Slaughterhouse Five*. But in several ways, it is different. Billy was cast about, emerging at one moment of time after another in random order. What I want to share is a story about how I became unstuck from the idea that there is only one reality and that it exists independent of my perception of it. I don't want to make this sound overly philosophical and metaphysical…. but unfortunately, it is. That is why I want to share all of this with you in a story.

We could start the story just about anywhere, and in fact with anyone; but I want to start this story with me, sitting in Washington Square just a few weeks ago, only a few blocks from where I live in Philadelphia. I went there to read on a hot summer day, and of course I was reading Kurt Vonnegut's *Slaughterhouse Five*. The way the novel moves back and forth through time loosened my mind. Those are my favorite stories, the ones that support a loose and free relationship with the familiar reality we are so accustomed to accept as the fact of the matter.

I was just sitting on a bench reading from my kindle when I noticed a woman walking towards me on the other side of the park. She was attractive with her long hair pulled tightly back and hanging down below her shoulder blades.

She was wearing a white pantsuit that included white slacks and a white vest worn over a flower print shirt. It struck me as an odd wardrobe choice on such a hot day. She walked with a sense of purpose and as she got closer, I could see just how attractive she was. Her eyes were big and round, her lips were bright red. The thing that stood out most to me was that she was wheeling a small suitcase with her. It was a white suitcase with a bold flower design on it. It was only an overnight bag, and I wondered where she was going with that at 10:30 in the morning. She walked straight to the park bench immediately to my right and sat down as I continued to read my book.

Then I heard her speak, but I was so immersed in reading that I hadn't heard what she said. I looked toward her, and she spoke again. "Do you want some gum?" she said, holding her hand toward me with a package of chewing gum in it.

"No, but thank you," I replied. Now this really did seem strange. After all, it was the middle of the COVID-19 pandemic. We were all wearing face masks to protect each other. It wasn't exactly the time I was likely to accept a stick of chewing gum. I wonder what would have happened if I had accepted. A whole alternative reality would have unfolded from the one I am telling you about now, but no sense wondering about it. There are always infinite alternative realities that simultaneously exist, but in human form only one will unfold for us.

As I continued to read, I was slightly distracted by this woman's presence. She kept looking at her phone, almost as if it were a mirror that she was using to admire how she looked. For a while I thought she was having a video call, but she never seemed to talk. She just stared into the phone. Occasionally she got up and walked a few hundred feet in a circle and sat down again. Then she wheeled her bag to a different bench and sat down. She seemed to be waiting for something, but I don't know what. Every now and again I would look up at her at exactly the same moment that she would be looking at me. Our eyes would briefly lock, and we would nod and smile to each other. After an hour or so it was time for me to leave so I could get home for a conference call. As I left the park, I made sure to walk past the woman and offer a friendly "goodbye" to her.

"Goodbye," she returned with a big smile. I took one last look at that white, hard-sided overnight bag with the big pink flowers on it before I walked away.

That woman was on my mind for the rest of the day. Yes, in part, it was because she was attractive and had initiated some minimal amount of contact with me. But more than that, it was the overly formal way she was dressed, the overnight bag she wheeled around, and especially the way she was interacting with her phone, that kept me wondering who she was and what she was doing in the park that morning.

I was still thinking about her when I returned to the park the next morning to read again. Reading in the park was becoming a habit of mine. I arrived slightly later than the day before. It was almost noon by the time I started hunting for the best place to sit. I took a bench not too far from where I had been the morning before, and as I sat down, I was thinking about the woman in the white pantsuit and part of me was hoping that she would come back again today.

Once again, I was reading *Slaughterhouse Five*. Actually, I was engrossed in reading because the book was drawing to a close and I was eager to see how the story, as disjointed from time as it was, would come to a conclusion. Suddenly, I saw someone out of the corner of my eye. I looked up, perhaps hoping that it was her again, but it wasn't. It was another woman. This woman was African American, with caramel colored skin. She was also very attractive, perhaps a little taller than the woman in the white pantsuit. This new woman was wearing a one-piece outfit. The material was light and patterned with wavy brown, black, orange, and yellow stripes. She was also wheeling a hard-sided overnight bag. This time the bag was black, but it had similar large, bold pink flowers printed on it.

As the woman in the striped one piece sat down just two benches to my right, I couldn't help feeling that unstuck-from-reality feeling that I often get. Was this a completely different woman? Who just happened to be wheeling a similar suitcase and wearing similarly overly formal attire for the day? Were these women real at all? Maybe they were figments of my imagination. Maybe I was the only one seeing them. Maybe they were being created in my mind. These thoughts were moving through me when suddenly the lady pulled out her phone and started staring at it in the same exact way that the woman the day before had. Just like the pantsuit woman, she was looking at it as if she were on a video call, but without ever speaking. If she were holding a mirror you would assume that she was checking her makeup - over and over again.

I was overcome by an urge to walk right up to her and say hello. I wanted to find out who she was and what she was doing. I especially needed to know if she was associated with the woman from the day before. How is it possible that two women could have such strikingly similar mannerisms, styles of dress, and an almost identical hard-sided overnight bag? They were also both strikingly attractive. I wondered if they were part of some high-end escort service, but somehow, I knew the truth was much more bizarre than that.

By now, I could hardly read a thing. I was completely distracted by my desire to speak with her and find out more about her. But how could I do that? "Hi, are you part of some classy escort service with the woman that was here yesterday?" I don't think that would work. "Hi, can I ask you what you are doing here with an overnight bag?" Only slightly better.

Then while I was looking in her direction she looked up and we caught eyes. "Hi," I said clearly. She looked down without acknowledging me. So that settled that, I wasn't going to talk with her. The mystery would be left unsolved. But at least I could let go of the whole thing and get back to reading. Billy Pilgrim was just now emerging onto what looked like a lunar landscape, but only yesterday it had been the beautiful city of Dresden before it was bombed along with all of its inhabitants in World War II. The novel is a condemnation of war. And it is an enduring classic because it manages to convey a deep feeling of futility. No one wins in war. Nothing you do, or can do, will make any real difference. It is a horror that leads to more horror and everything you do in an attempt to oppose it will be equally doomed to contributing to what can only be a horrible ending.

After an hour I had finished the novel and I got up to walk away. I did not say goodbye to the beautiful African American woman in the striped one piece. I just walked home, still thinking about the two women I had encountered on consecutive days.

The next morning, after getting up, having some coffee and writing an introduction for the new book I had just finished writing, I left earlier than usual for the park. I was finished with *Slaughterhouse Five*, and now I was reading *Lost Horizon*, the novel that introduced the fictional land of Shangri-La, a secret realm deep in the mountains of Tibet. Of course, as I walked to the park I wondered if I would see either of the two women from the days before. I did not. There were many people in the park, but neither of the two women were there. I read for a while and then left.

Later in the afternoon, I decided to take a walk along the Delaware River. It was a beautiful day. The sun was out and pleasantly warm. All along the river there were people walking in pairs or small groups. Most, but not all, were wearing face masks to protect against the spread of the COVID-19 pandemic, and as best they could, people were maintaining some distance from one another. Most of the people around me were African American and most seemed joyful, light, and free. It was refreshing to share this human moment in the middle of such challenging times. There was a sense of being unified in the experience of rejoicing together in the bright sunshine with the grey blue water of the wide river slowing sliding past us.

I walked all the way from Spruce Street to Chestnut before heading away from the coast and onto the walking bridge that spanned across the highway below. I walked over the wide brick bridge, which was wide enough for cars, but closed to traffic. Once on the other side, I walked west on Chestnut street and in my mind, I was deciding which street I wanted to walk south on to head home.

In the middle of such mundane thoughts and still feeling the happy inner glow from the experience of communion along the river, I saw a third woman with a flowered overnight suitcase. This one was walking toward me on the opposite side of Chestnut street. She was also African American and also wearing a one-piece jumpsuit, but I could see that it was a different woman than yesterday. Her jumpsuit was a dark blue with a faint white pattern on it. She was wheeling the same white suitcase with pink flowers that the first woman in white had been wheeling. I couldn't help but stare. She was, like the previous two women, strikingly attractive.

It wasn't until she walked past me, and I turned around to watch her walk away that something snapped in my mind. As I watched her walk past, I saw that her suitcase, which on one side had pink flowers on a white background, had on the other side a black background with the same pink flowers printed on it. The suitcase that was being wheeled by these three beautiful women was the same one! I had only seen one side of it on the first encounter, and then the other side yesterday, and now I was seeing both sides.

I turned without thinking and followed her. She walked halfway across the walking bridge and then sat down on a bench. She took out her phone and started looking into it in the exact same way that the other two women had. This was a message. I was getting another message. These were not real women, or perhaps I should say they were more than real, they were hyper-real, born out of a confluence of what we call reality, and the higher-dimensional reality that coexists with it. I was the vehicle of confluence, the nexus point. I was the instrument through which higher dimensional realities were revealing something here on earth as these three beautiful women wheeling the same hard-sided flower print suitcase. They were a sign, a symbol. I just had to figure out what they were telling me.

You see, these women are not real in the normal sense, but don't worry, nothing else is either. We have been taught that reality is a three-dimensional space that is filled with material objects that interact and change over time. It isn't. Reality is a convergence of many dimensions of possibility that come into being as they come into contact. The reality that we know and experience is more like a whirlpool on the surface of a river than it is a solid reality of sticks and stones. In the water of the river, currents converge and swirl into a circle that becomes visible on the surface. The whirlpool looks like something separate from the water, but it is not. In an analogous way, the potentials of multiple dimensions collide and emerge on the surface of our reality in the form of our familiar three-dimensional universe. Like a whirlpool on the surface of a river, it swirls for a moment or two and then disappears. You and I and everything else are a part of this swirling temporary emergence of being.

But these three ladies are something else, and I don't know exactly what they are. Our reality is like a whirlpool that emerges out of a confluence of dimensional realities that create a relatively stable experience, but sometimes a new dimensional possibility passes through, you could even say a rogue possibility, one that has liberated itself even from the laws that bind trans-dimensional interactions. The encounter with such a rogue potentiality creates strange occurrences. They are responsible for what we call paranormal and supernatural phenomena. Of course, these occurrences would be more accurately described as trans-dimensional, but that is not how we understand them at present.

When I see three beautiful ladies, on three consecutive days, wheeling the same suitcase and staring into their cell-phones in the same odd way, I know I am encountering a trans-dimensional phenomenon. Trans-dimensional crossings are multilayered, mutually influencing events. They are not just things that happen to us. These otherworldly possibilities don't just stumble though our universe, they are invited in. They are called into the encounter, usually by unconscious means. In this case, I must have called these three ladies into being. Otherwise they would not have been able to appear. I don't want to leave you with the impression that these ladies only exist in my mind. Not at all. Once they are called into being, they will exist for everyone to see and interact with, but they will have a special ontologically symbiotic relationship to me. Since it was my unconscious mind that created the doorway for them to pass through, their existence here is intimately linked with me. And, conversely, once they appear, they shift my karmic destiny, and become an unavoidable part of my unfolding future. I call them into being, and their shape and destiny will always be linked with me, but once they come into being my shape and my destiny will always be linked with theirs.

How do I know this? Well, I have had a good deal of experience with these things, but I will have to tell you a little more about my story to explain all that. Some things can't be understood outside of a story; well, in fact, nothing can be understood outside of a story, but some stories take longer to tell than others. To tell this story I am going to have to start a few decades earlier when my spiritual life was just beginning.

# CHAPTER TWO

I was standing on the street outside of a yoga studio in Cambridge, Massachusetts. Apparently, it was owned, or so I was told, by a famous yoga teacher. At the age of 28, this was about to be my very first time ever in a yoga studio. There were about forty people lined up at the door. We were waiting to participate in a satsang, a spiritual gathering with a teacher, offered by a young American guru whose book, *Real Life Happens Where You're Not Looking*, I had devoured on the same day that I had bought it two months before. It wasn't the first spiritual book I had read. By that time, I had been reading Buddhist, Sufi, and New Age books by the score for a couple of years. But I hadn't yet encountered the radical teachings of Advaita Vedanta, or as it was called in its imported Western version, Neo-Advaita.

The idea, as I understood it, was simple. You are already free and unlimited. And you are already divine, because divinity is all there is. Reality is one, or as the tradition puts it, non-dual or not-two. There is only consciousness and it is omnipresent, always already awake, forever free, and sacred. The big 'aha' that this tradition offers is the realization that all of our seeking for truth is the only thing that keeps us from realizing that the experience of life that we are having right now already contains the whole truth. This is it!

Every page of *Real Life Happens Where You're Not Look-*

*ing* presents a short teaching of this ancient realization. Each one points you to the immediate realization of truth and the futility of any path that insists on the insertion of time between you and that goal. "Stop wanting anything but what is," it told me. "Stop assuming that anything needs to happen at all. If you really want to be whole, complete and fulfilled, then be THAT right now, exactly as you are." It was a Saturday morning when I found the book on the shelf of a spiritual bookstore near where I lived in the suburbs of Boston. I started reading it sitting in my car in the parking lot. Two hours later I drove off. I was feeling light and happy. It all made so much sense.

I was running some errands that day because I had promised my wife that I would do some yard work. I stopped at the hardware store to pick up the things I needed to fix our broken picket fence. When I sat back down in my car, I picked up the book again. Two hours later I had read it all, except for two chapters which I had skipped. My vision was so clear. All of the colors of the world felt vivid and bright, and every line was crisp and clear. I had taken acid a few times when I was in college and this felt like a flashback, except it included only the most positive elements of an acid trip.

I looked at the photo of the author. He was a striking man named Johnny Free, although he was known as Dr. Free to his students. On the back cover of the book written over Dr. Free's photo was the sentence "If you really want what I got, it can be yours!" I really wanted what he 'got'. I really wanted what I had found in this book. I knew without any doubt that what I was reading about in this book was everything I had always wanted even if

I hadn't realized it. Over the next month I read the book over and over again, but there were two chapters that I always skipped. These two chapters explored the relationship with a spiritual teacher, but I had no interest in working with a spiritual teacher. The only stories I had heard about spiritual teachers were of duplicity and abuse, and I had no desire to experience either. But I couldn't help reading and rereading all the other chapters over and over again. Eventually, I went back to the same spiritual bookstore where I had found the book originally to see if Dr. Free had written other books.

As I walked into the doorway, I saw on the notice board a small poster with Dr. Free's face on it. Underneath the picture it said, "Stop wanting anything but what is." Dr. Free was going to be teaching at a yoga studio not too far from where I lived. The poster promised that he would show you where your Real Life is happening. I was astounded by my incredibly good luck. I stumbled upon his book just a month or so before and he happened to be coming to my neighborhood in another month. At the time, I didn't realize that Dr. Free traveled to teach at that yoga studio every six months or so, and I never would have guessed that for the next 21 years I would be organizing teaching events for him not only in Cambridge, but throughout the world. Not knowing any of that, I was simply astounded by my good fortune. Over the next four weeks I would reread *Real Life Happens Where You're Not Looking* another half dozen times, always skipping the two chapters on the student-teacher relationship.

That is how I came to be standing on the street outside of a yoga studio in Cambridge, Massachusetts with forty other people waiting for satsang to begin. I was a little nervous. I had seen a couple of spiritual teachers before, but this felt different. The people around me all seemed to know each other. It was a little odd, everyone was talking excitedly. They all seemed very friendly and in very good spirits. Every few minutes someone would come up to me and ask me my name and then, invariably, they would ask how I had heard of Dr. Free. I would tell them about reading his book and seeing the poster in the bookstore. One woman, a decade or so older than me, got very excited when I told her about how I had heard of Dr. Free.

"I put that poster up in the bookstore!" She exclaimed with a big grin. "I am so glad you told me that that's how you found out about this. I put up so many posters whenever Dr. Free comes and I often don't know if they help or not."

"Well this one helped me," I said before asking, "So, do you know Dr. Free?"

"Oh yes, I have been a student of Dr. Free for four years, ever since he first came back to America to teach."

"How did you first hear about him?" I asked.

"I was a member of the Boston Buddhist Meditation Society and we started hearing from our sister branch in the UK about this American teacher who had recently returned from India and was setting everyone on fire for liberation. The story was that a number of people had been catapulted into profound experiences of enlightened consciousness by this man."

"Is it true?" I asked innocently and eagerly.

"You're about to find out," she said nodding over my shoulder to point out that the door of the yoga studio was opening, and it was time to go in. The studio room was large enough to easily hold sixty of us on the floor. There were pillows and mats strewn about that we could use to sit on. The lighting was bright, and one wall was mirrored which made the room look twice as big as it was. There was a comfortable chair set up with a table and a vase of flowers and everyone started to arrange themselves around it. I sat down toward the back of the room. A moment later an older man sat on my left and then a pretty young woman sat next to me on the right. I had seen the man outside. He had seemed to know a lot of people and I assumed him to be one of the "community" members, so I was intimidated to talk to him. The girl to my right looked about as uncertain as I felt about the whole thing.

"Hi, is this your first time seeing Dr. Free, too?" I asked.

"Yes," she said with a smile.

"Me too. Have you ever been to anything like this before?"

"You mean a satsang? Yes, many. I've seen a few other Advaita Non-Dual teachers. How about you?"

"I've seen Thich Nhat Hanh and Ram Dass. That's about it really."

"So, you've never seen a Non-Dual teacher?" she remarked.

"Not yet."

"Well, this should be different then." She said just as I saw that Dr. Free had walked into the room through a small back door and was walking toward the chair with the side table and the flowers. The chatter in the room hushed and by the time he sat in the chair the room was in silence. Dr. Free sat with his feet on the floor and his back straight.

He closed his eyes and sat very still. After a few moments it seemed that everyone else had closed their eyes, so I did, too. We sat for a long time, or at least it seemed that way. Then suddenly, I heard Dr. Free say in a surprisingly meek and high-pitched voice, "Ok, I'm ready to start."

I opened my eyes and saw that he was looking back and forth across the room. He was not a big man, but there was something about his mannerism and his energy that was intimidating. No one spoke for a while until someone finally broke the awkward silence.

"On what authority do you teach? You have no teacher, no lineage. Why do you feel you are qualified to teach at all?" asked a rather angry looking man sitting toward the back of the room and on my right. It struck me as a very unfair and demanding question. Of course, I had no idea what the background story was behind it. If I had known more about Dr. Free at the time, it wouldn't have struck me as being so undeserved as it did on that night.

"Believe me," Dr. Free began, "I would never do this if I didn't feel that I had the authority to do it."

"Why should I believe you?" the angry man said.

"You probably shouldn't," said Dr. Free confidently. "But tell me, why did you come here? Was it just to ask challenging questions?"

"To prove that you're a fake!" said the now angrier man loudly.

"Are you satisfied?" Dr. Free asked. "Have I sufficiently proven myself to be a fake so that you can stop asking questions and let the evening move on?"

Dr. Free, by offering no defense, had solidified the sympathies of the room in his direction. A number of people were now glaring back at the angry man in an effort to get him to stop.

"Yes, you have satisfied me. I don't need to stay for any more of this." And with that the angry man stormed out the door and five or six people followed. I had no idea what had just happened. I had no background to understand any of it.

The next few questions were similarly challenging. There was a question about his lack of lineage and whether he was just making things up. There was a question about how he obviously was not enlightened – which was not obvious to me – and then there was a question about a book that had been written by a detractor. Eventually, Dr. Free said that he was going to leave the room and that he would not come back until everyone who had come only to be difficult left. He got up and slowly walked out the door and two people, whom I could only assume were close students, followed after him.

Now the tension in the room was very high. Some people started demanding that the people who had asked challenging questions leave, which they did not, and the tension just increased.

Then others did start leaving. The pretty woman to my left whispered to me. "I am not staying here. This isn't satsang, this is crazy." And then she got up and left the room. By this time, ten or so people had left. Finally, all of the people who had asked challenging questions had left the room and the energy calmed down. We sat in silence for what seemed like another long time before Dr. Free returned.

"Ok, that feels better." He said with a triumphant smile. "Does anyone have a real question?"

People started asking questions; real questions, I guess. Questions about spiritual practice and meditation. Questions about enlightenment and the nature of the self. Dr. Free answered each question authoritatively and definitively. He seemed very confident and very certain. I didn't understand a word of it. Of course, I understood all the English words, just not in the order they were being used. I felt very confused. I desperately wanted to ask a question, but I was too afraid to speak. I kept starting to raise my hand up, but it would never get higher than the shoulder of the person in front of me. It was as if it were hitting an invisible forcefield. I just couldn't make it rise any higher so that Dr. Free would see it. I kept wondering why I was so afraid. I was looking at the clock realizing that my time was running out. I knew that I had to ask him a question, but I also knew that I would not.

"Ok, that's it for tonight," he finally said. Then he sat up straight again with his feet on the floor and closed his eyes. I had missed my chance to ask Dr. Free a question, but I was relieved to be free from the pressure of trying. Dr. Free was actually leading another satsang the next night and another the night after that. I hadn't necessarily intended to go to all three satsangs, but now I decided that I would. I decided that during the next night's satsang, I wouldn't worry at all about speaking. I would just go and listen as carefully as I could to hear what Dr. Free was saying. If I still wanted to speak to him, I would do it on the third night.

I arrived even earlier at the yoga studio the next night. I wanted to sit close to Dr. Free, so I arrived about an hour before the satsang was scheduled to start. There were still about twelve people already in line. I saw the older man who had sat on my left the night before.

"Good, you're back. I wasn't sure. You seemed to be having a hard time deciding if you wanted to talk to the doctor or not last night," he said as I moved to stand behind him in the line. "My name is Bob, by the way." He thrust out his hand and I took it. He had a firm grip and he shook vigorously.

"I'm Brian," I said and then added, "Yeah, I wanted to come back and hear some more. Tonight, I think I'll just listen and not bother about speaking."

"Sounds like a good idea," he said with a wink.

That evening I sat on the floor as close as I could to Dr. Free's chair, and I looked up and stared at him the entire night. I listened to every word. One person after another would ask a question and each answer was a different variation of the same sentiment. In essence, it was the exact same insight that was contained in each page of *Real Life Happens Where You're Not Looking* - this is it!

At one point a young man very earnestly and passionately expressed how much he wanted spiritual freedom and nothing else. He was pleading with Dr. Free to show him how to liberate himself from the prison of the mind. It struck me as equal parts beautiful and pathetic. The man's eyes were practically bulging out of his head. They were red and watering. His hands were gesturing wildly and there was a pleading tone in his voice that veered into childlike whines.

"Please, Dr. Free, I want to be free!" the man said. "How do I free myself from the torment of my mind? How do I see clearly beyond all of my mind's fears and concerns?"

"Ignore them," Dr. Free said quietly.

"I can't, they're too loud! They never stop. My mind is always chattering at me."

"I thought you wanted to be free?" Dr. Free said.

"I do!" the man said, almost angrily now.

"Then do it now."

"Do what?"

"Be free."

"Yes, that's what I want, but I don't know how."

"You don't want to be free." Dr. Free said challengingly. "You want me to liberate you. I can't do that. No one can do that. No one can free you because you are already free. All you have to do is accept that this is already the freedom that you are pretending to seek. You don't want freedom. You want a path to freedom. You want me to show you how to get there, as if it is not already here. You are trying to trick me into giving you a method that will lead you to freedom. There is no such method. Freedom is now. If I give you a method, if I tell you to do something now so that you will be free later, I will be validating your belief that this is not already it. I will be working against freedom, not for it. There is no way to be free except by being free. If you really want to be free, then be it and be done with any concern about it."

"How do I do that?" the man asked desperately.

"You give up all your concerns about being free or not being free. Embrace the truth that this is it and move on. Just do it. It doesn't take any time. Let go of your concerns about being free right now!" Dr. Free spoke loudly as he stared intently into the man's eyes.

I was watching the man's face as he heard Dr. Free's final command. The anger and desperation in his eyes gave way.

His eyes widened in wonder. He seemed to be staring off now into a space behind and beyond Dr. Free. Tears were streaming down his cheeks. He started sobbing loudly.

"I'm so sorry. It is all right here. It was always right here. There was never anything in the way. My mind is not a problem, only my fascination with it ever was," he said through loud gulps of air.

"Yes, now you are seeing with eyes cleared of the illusion of needing more time. You are open to the truth of what is." And with that Dr. Free turned generally to everyone else sitting in the audience. "You see? You can do this the hard way or the easy way. You can simply let go and be free - that's the easy way. Or you can pretend to be all tied up and bound and slowly hack away at the imaginary ropes around your body - that is the hard way. Do us all a favor and choose the easy way."

That was a particularly dramatic interaction, but the whole night was filled with similar ones. Sometimes they ended in someone's realization of something wonderful that no one else could see. Sometimes they ended in frustration. At one point about halfway through the evening, Dr. Free was looking around the room between questions. He suddenly looked straight at me. There was an intensity to his unmoving gaze as it met my eyes.

"What is your name?" he said.

"Brian." I answered.

Then he moved on and took another question. It wasn't much, but contact had been made. I was resolved that tomorrow night I would come back and I would ask my question. I would take my turn in the spotlight and try my luck at Dr. Free's liberation game.

# CHAPTER THREE

I arrived very early the next night and went to the cafe next door because no one else had arrived at the yoga studio. I sat in a seat facing the window of the cafe so that I could watch as people arrived for the satsang with Dr. Free. Bob, my new friend from the night before, arrived first. He opened the glass door with a key and walked in. He was wheeling a small suitcase with him. I saw him walk through the lobby before he disappeared through the door of the studio. A few minutes later two women arrived. They were middle aged, in their forties or fifties like Bob. They were wheeling even bigger suitcases, and each carried a large grocery bag that appeared to be full of something. They knocked at the door and Bob came out to unlock the door and let them in. All three of them disappeared into the studio.

I was shocked to see that the next person to arrive was Dr. Free himself. He was alone and walked up to the outside door and just stood there with his hands on his hips. I thought he must be waiting for someone to come and unlock the door for him, but after five minutes no one had come. I jumped up out of my seat, left my coffee steaming hot on the table, and walked outside and across the street.

"Hello, Dr. Free." I said excitedly from a few feet away. He turned as I approached, and I suddenly realized that I had no idea what to say. "Are you waiting to get in?"

"No, no, my friend. I am trying to decide if I want to

go in or not."

"Really?" I asked.

"Well yes, in over twenty years of teaching it has only been twice that I didn't go in, but it has happened."

"You mean, you just decided that you didn't want to teach on those nights?"

"Not really. You see, before I go in, I ask for permission to teach. I wait to get an answer. It is almost always a yes, but twice no answer came, and I took that to be 'no.'"

"Do you actually hear a voice that answers?"

"No, actually if the answer is yes a cascade of light sprinkles down into the top of my head. It feels delightful." He then nodded upward toward the sky. "I think they are up there you know - the ones that watch over me - on some other planet or maybe an orbiting satellite - I can't tell. They make sure it is all safe for me before I go in."

"I see." I said unconvincingly.

"Don't worry, it will all make sense soon enough," he said with a wink. Then he paused and looked up toward the sky. "There they are. All clear." And with that he took a key out of his pocket, opened the door and went in. "See you in a few minutes," he said as he walked through the lobby and disappeared into the yoga studio.

A few minutes later people started to arrive. I said hello to a few of them and a few said hello to me, but I didn't want to get into any conversations, so I kept to myself. I was feeling a little nervous. I was determined to ask Dr. Free my question today and our brief encounter didn't do anything to calm my apprehensions. After twenty minutes, Bob appeared from behind the studio door and unlocked the front door to let everyone in. I said hi to Bob as I walked past, and he smiled wide. I sat on the floor, in the second row from the front. I was sitting on a yoga cushion just to the left of Dr. Free's chair. We all sat in silence waiting.

As I sat there, I contemplated what Dr. Free had said about the beings from some other planet, or an orbiting satellite. I hadn't read anything like that in his book. I wonder if he meant it, or if he was joking with me. Maybe he was testing to see how gullible I was. Or maybe he was serious. Maybe he thinks he is being guided by alien beings. Maybe, in fact, he was being guided by alien beings. How did I know?

Dr. Free came into the room and sat down in his chair at the front of the room. I was about seven feet from his feet. He wore bright white socks and black dress pants. His shirt was a bright flower print of reds and yellows and he had a black vest over that. He sat still, took a long glance around the room and then closed his eyes. We sat together with him that way for what seemed like thirty to forty minutes. Then I heard his voice say, "Ok, I'm ready to start." My hand shot straight up into the air. I had prepared myself to raise my hand as soon as he said he was ready to start. I didn't want to let anyone else speak first, because I was afraid that I would lose my nerve.

"Yes," he said looking straight at me.

I took a deep breath and asked the question I had been preparing to ask for three days. "A couple of months ago I bought your book, *Real Life Happens Where You're Not Looking,* and everything in it is truer than anything else I've ever heard. But where do I find the faith to give everything to it and know that it is going to turn out OK?"

He paused a moment as if weighing the odds. Then

he looked sternly and deeply into my eyes and said, "Who says it's going to turn out OK? It could end up a complete mess! If you knew it was all going to turn out OK, you wouldn't need any faith, would you? No, you wouldn't, because you'd already have a guarantee!"

Something dislodged between me and my mind. I felt light and free as if I was floating in air. He kept on talking, but I could no longer hear him speak. I heard the sound coming out of his mouth, but it was just meaningless noise now. I wasn't listening to what he was saying. I suddenly saw how true it was. I wasn't trying to find faith. I wanted a guarantee. I wanted there to be some safe way to be so that a positive outcome would be assured. And it wasn't just in this instance. I saw my whole life was one huge attempt to find security. I was trying to figure out how to live life right. I was looking for a path to a fulfilling and happy life that couldn't go wrong. But now, in this strange light-hearted moment, I saw clearly that there was no such thing as a right way to live. Or at least, there was no way to know what it was ahead of time.

You live life once and it turns out the way it turns out. There is no way to live that is any more or less assured to have a positive outcome as any other. Life is always a fifty-fifty gamble. You live it once and eventually, as it comes to an end, you are either going to feel satisfied with the life that you have lived, or you are going to wish you could start over. You are either going to leave this world satisfied or regretful. And there is no way to know until that final exit which it will be. You could live your entire life following the rules and trying to play it safe, like I had been my whole life, and that could end up leaving you wishing you had taken more risks. You could live on the edge and end up wishing you had been more conservative. Every life, and every other life, is a fifty-fifty gamble.

My head was swirling. There was no way to know ahead of time. There was no way to figure life out and get it right. You could only live, but how was I going to live? If I couldn't figure out how to do it right, then what was I going to do? How do you decide anything, if everything is a fifty-fifty gamble? I had always thought I was doing a pretty good job at life. I had a good career, a lovely wife, a white house with a white picket fence and two cars in the garage. I was making good money and so was my wife. We were a DINK household - double income, no kids - and we were enjoying it. Suddenly, I realized that this life was no more likely to lead to satisfaction than any other. It was the life that my society told me would be most satisfying, but just because your culture tells you it is, doesn't make it so.

Then everything stopped. All the noise, all the movement, everything, it all instantaneously came to a dead stop - a total stand still. It was like in a movie when time freezes. I couldn't hear anything, and everything around me was frozen stiff. I looked up and even Dr. Free was frozen. He was leaning toward me with his mouth open and both his hands were raised in a gesture of emphasis. The people around me were all frozen in different expressions of rapt attention. Time had stopped. Then I heard someone say "Hey!" from behind me. I looked around and saw that it was Dr. Free standing by the back door waving his arm for me to join him. I looked forward again and Dr. Free was still seated in his frozen position. I looked back and he was still standing at the door waving me over. I sat still and

looked around for a long minute or two and then I got up
and walked over to Dr. Free, stepping over and around the
deathly still individuals scattered about on the floor.

As I got near to Dr. Free, he walked out through the door
and across the floor of the lobby and out into the night air. I
followed him and as I walked outside, I saw a young couple
who had evidently been walking arm in arm past the yoga
studio when time froze. She was looking up into his face,
hanging heavily on his right arm. He was in the middle of a
big step forward and seemed to be looking up at the starry
sky. Just beyond them a big black limousine was parked and
Dr. Free walked up to it and opened the door. "Climb in,"
he said as I approached him. I didn't even think about it. I
just did as he said and got into the limo. Dr. Free got in next
and sat opposite me. Then the limo drove off slowly.

"Where are we going?" I asked absentmindedly.

"I'm not sure yet. It seems that you haven't decided," he
responded looking at me intensely.

"Is it up to me where we go?" I asked.

"Of course. This is your dream, after all."

"Oh, that explains it." I said looking away from Dr.
Free and then, speaking to myself I said, "I'm asleep in bed.
I never went to satsang. I just dreamed that I did and now
I am here dreaming about a conversation with Dr. Free." I
closed my eyes, screwed up my face and tried to wake up. A
grunting sound came out of my mouth from the exertion.
Dr. Free laughed.

"What are you laughing at?" I asked angrily.

"Well, technically you have the power to end this if
you want, but not with that kind of effort. You can push so
hard that you give yourself a hernia and it won't accomplish

a thing."

"Why don't you tell me how to end this then?" I demanded.

"I've been telling you how to do that all night," he said. "Everything I teach is about one thing - how to wake yourself up from the dream."

"How do I wake myself up and get back to being in my bed?"

"You aren't in bed."

"Back to satsang in the studio then."

"That would be the opposite direction of waking up. You see, you are actually a lot more awake here than you were in the studio. In fact, you're a lot more awake right now than you've ever been, but you're still less than halfway there. You've got a lot more waking up to do before you're done," Dr. Free explained.

"I don't know what you're talking about, but I want to get out of here." I turned and opened the limo door. What I saw made me jump backwards in my seat. The street was gone. The car was floating at least a thousand feet off the ground. I could see the yoga studio like a toy in a model of a city.

"You might want to get out of here, but evidently your unconscious wants you to stay," said Dr. Free, gesturing with his head toward the open door and the ground below. "If you consciously and unconsciously wanted to go back to the way things were, you would have opened the door and walked straight back into the studio and started the whole thing up again. You wouldn't even remember this. Clearly you do want to wake up or you wouldn't have gotten this far in the first place. And now seeing how you've blocked your own escape, it is clear to me that you are going to go all the way with this. That is all I needed to see. Take a good look around, you won't remember any of this in a moment." Dr. Free made a sweeping gesture with his hand.

...

Suddenly, I realized that this life was no more likely to lead to satisfaction than any other. It was the life that my society told me would be most satisfying, but just because your culture tells you it is, doesn't make it so. I looked up and saw that Dr. Free was still looking down at me from his chair. Evidently, he had been talking for some time. I didn't remember anything he had said, but now I heard him clearly.

"Listen to me. The part of you that wants a guarantee is the part that is getting its head dragged to a chopping block. What I am offering here is a one-way ticket. If you get on this train, you never come back!"

I felt so strange. I didn't know whether to laugh or cry. I had no idea what was happening to me. I felt like I was going to pass out.

"Anyone else?" Dr. Free said, scanning around the room for another raised hand. I heard him call on someone and I heard the sound of a different voice asking a question. Dr. Free began to answer, but I couldn't understand anything that was being said.

I was somewhere else. I was in the middle of a life, a life that was just as likely to turn out a mess as anything else. I was like the ball on a spinning roulette wheel with no idea where I would land. And so was everyone else. Everyone trying to get it right, trying to play by the rules, or trying to get it right by breaking the rules. Or not trying at all so they could avoid the game. And all of them had exactly the same odds of winning or losing. Nothing we do, or could do, changes the odds of life. It is always a fifty-fifty bet. It will turn out to be satisfying or it won't. It will turn out to be worth it or it won't. I felt listless. Why even try if the game was stacked against you? Why bother? The most logical thing to do was give up, but for some reason the thought of giving up made me angry.

"I won't be beaten down by life. I won't let the odds stop me." I thought, and suddenly I realized exactly how I would play the game. I understood that there was one way to play that would guarantee victory. I would play exactly the way I wanted to play. I would live exactly the life I thought was most worthwhile. Sure, there would still be a fifty-fifty chance of the whole thing turning out a big mess. But even if it did, even if it turned out totally rotten, at least I would know that I had given it my best shot. I had chosen my own life. I had lived according to what I thought was best. I had taken the conscious risk to choose. So even if it did turn out a mess, I would know I had given it everything. At least I would not get to that messy end and feel like I had been duped by someone. The blame would all be mine - and that I realized was the trick. If you wanted to be free, you had to take full responsibility for the consequences of your life. In the end, there would be no one to blame, but me. I was ready. I knew then and there that I would devote myself to being spiritually free. I would live my own life and I would accept any consequences that occurred as a result of my choices. I was taking full control of my life, and at the very same time I was surrendering my entire life over to spiritual freedom. Nothing else would ever matter to me.

This reminded me of two stories about Viking warriors. There is the more famous story about how Vikings would burn their own boats as they got off on the shore of a land they intended to conquer. They would do this so that retreat was impossible. Once they got off and burned the boats behind them there was no way home. They had to conquer or die trying. But there is another story someone once told me that is even more intriguing to me. It seems that the night before a big battle, Vikings would gather for a religious ceremony. They would dance and sing and go into deep trance states. In these deep states they would embrace the fact that they had already died in tomorrow's battle. They were not just accepting that they might die, they were embracing the fact that they were going to die, and they had no doubt about that fact. So, once they began fighting in the battle, they had nothing to lose. They knew they were going to die; they just didn't know exactly how or when, but they knew it would be today, in this battle. In that state of mind, there was nothing at all for them to defend. They could be totally, wholeheartedly committed to the attack because there was no sense protecting a life that was already lost.

In some analogous fashion, I felt that my life was now over. I was going to devote my entire life, from this moment to the very last, to only one thing - spiritual freedom. I was going to find spiritual freedom, or I was going to die trying. There was no reason to try to protect or retain anything about my life the way it was. Everything was going to be different now.

# CHAPTER FOUR

Whenever I wake up, I wake up in the middle. In the middle of a life that is already in progress. I wasn't there at the start, but I am now. I meet people and I seem to know who they are, but I only remember them as far back as the moment when the dream began. I don't remember yesterday, or the day before that, or last year or anything else that happened before I woke up. I feel like I have a past. The people I meet treat me as if I do. But I don't remember anything further back than the moment I arrived in the dream. I wonder about the person who was there before I woke up, was that really me or someone else?

Soft bubbles float up from the center of my stomach as I look over the glassy surface of a pale grey lake. The bubbles become cold with fear as they ripen and rise up my spine into the back of my neck before exiting through the top of my head.

How did I get here? This is an important place. I think. I have to remember how I got here, but I can't. I don't even remember how to remember anymore. How do I recall something?

I could never have predicted what my life is like now. I had heard about presence, and enlightenment, and multi-dimensionality. I had read all the books and went to the retreats; but none of what I had previously thought has anything to do with this. I could never have imagined being severed, as I am now, from both the past and the future. No one could have imagined this. It is unimaginable.

You can't plan for your arrival in the eternal, all-knowing present. You can't do anything to get there because it isn't a place you can get to. You don't exist there. It just is. That ever-perfect moment is completely free of any idea of me. It just is.

The pond is so still. Without ripples. I am so close to the water. My vision is skimming right along the glassy surface. How do you turn to see behind you if you have no head? Awareness can't turn around, it only sees forward.

But now it is turning. My desire to see what is behind me is shifting the vantage point of awareness. Slowly my line of sight moves to the left. Of course, I know what's behind me because I am there, too. It is only a habit of perception that forces the need for this painstakingly slow feat of perceptual maneuvering. If I had more faith in the omnidirectional nature of awareness, I would already know what I now have to wait to see.

Seeing behind me now, I am about 50 feet from the edge of the pond. I see a small building that I know is a zendo, a meditation house belonging to a Japanese Roshi. I can see the old man. I can see his bald head and long beard. I don't know if I am remembering him or seeing him. I don't know if there is any difference in reality between remembering and seeing. When you can see always and everywhere at the same time the distinction of remembering versus knowing disappears.

How would I have guessed that the total absorption of presence would feel so much like prison. Who would have known that being everywhere all at once, would be the same as being nowhere? Having everything you could ever want is the same as having nothing at all. Nothing could prepare me, or anyone else, for this moment, for this ever-lasting encounter with that which is always unprecedented. Nothing can lead you to this moment because it leaves no space at all for there having been any past that could ever have led up to it. It is is. Only.

I had read so much about awakening. I had dreamed about Oneness with the infinite universe. Now I see clearly that everything I had read was all lies. But of course, any-thing that anyone could say about this impossible possibili-ty would have been a lie. It wasn't anyone's fault. They were engaged in a noble, although arguably misguided attempt, to express the inexpressible. So, in a sense they weren't lying at all. If everything is a lie, then there can be no truth. So then, everything is also true.

Well-intentioned though they may be, all of the en-lightened teachers, writers, priests, and poets were all sharing misconceived ideas about the inconceivable. How could they not be? I am sure they knew it at the time but couldn't think of anything better to do. It isn't their fault. Anyone who was to stumble upon the essence of essence, the ground of the ground, would feel equally and unavoid-ably compelled to try to share it, even if they knew they couldn't. I will do the same. I know it. In fact, I already am.

But right now, I am stuck. Imprisoned in a present that has no past and no future. The prison of the infinite and eternal nature of reality. I cannot escape because there is nowhere and no one to escape to.

My choice seems simple enough. I can rest and fall asleep one last time. I can let the darkness fall over me and sleep for just this one forever moment. I can die into the eternal, or I can reconstruct a sense of past and future, here and there, self and other. I can return to the world of time and space and the company of others; and doing so I will feel compelled to take up a task that cannot be accomplished.

But why would I return? What would I return to? Who would I return as? Wouldn't it be much simpler to become one with the infinite universe right here and now? Why go back?

Ahh, but it is already too late for these questions. The mere fact that this ridiculous contemplation is even taking place tells me that I have already decided to come back. I am already coming back, or I wouldn't even be able to have these thoughts. This very conversation about whether I should return or not is itself the first step in coming back. A step that was taken by someone I already don't remember. I am already on my way back to the world of living amnesia.

Why? Why come back? Who decided that? Why not remain merged with the unending explosion of love and bliss?

I am seeing again the movement of change. On the return from oblivion, difference - the sense of distinction between one thing and another - is the first perception to return. Close behind is change; and change automatically brings time along with it. Time brings a sense of memory and that gives birth to the past and along with that the idea of a future inevitably comes. From here there is a brief rush of conceptions that label the world. Right now, I cannot remember anything, and I cannot imagine anything. All I can perceive is what is in front of me, I will enjoy this moment suspended as it is outside of time. It won't last long. I can already begin to remember the turning. The past creeps into awareness and I see a growing sense of anticipation of the future. Time is returning.

One scene, the steely grey blue surface of the lake extending in all directions and a small wooden zendo on the shore. Seeing is all that is happening. Seeing and the beginning of knowing. Knowing that this is the surface of a lake or perhaps a pond, and that that is a zendo. And the beginning of remembering. Remembering the Roshi with his bald head and beard. Who is the Roshi? And who is the one that remembers the Roshi?

The unitive moment is the most peaceful, the most beautiful, and the most tedious experience that could be. There is never anything wrong in the eternal present. There is never anything right either. In that singularity there just is. There is no difference, no distinction and certainly no change. It is a feeling of love and bliss, but not any kind you can imagine. The love and bliss at the center of reality is like a movie that is playing without a screen. It is there shining into the emptiness but without a reflecting surface there is no way to know it. It is pure love and pure bliss. It is pure radiance, forever radiating away from anyone who could ever possibly experience it.

Those who wish to remain forever in that love-bliss can do so simply by giving up any sense of preference for anything, especially for experiencing love and bliss. If you want nothing, then you will always already have it. You can rest there forever. But, if you want anything at all, the force of wanting, even wanting love and bliss, will move you away from where you always already are.

It would be so easy to stay. So easy to not want anything but this. Yet, I am already returning. I will not stay. I don't know why, but I am coming back. The descent has already begun. I will return. I will remember. I will bring with me a meaningless message about a possibility without any hope of being shared. I don't know why, and right now I don't know how, but I will return.

Remember. Remember. Remember.

...

The first thing I notice is her hair. It is auburn colored. Where it is thick it is so dark it is nearly black. But where it is thin and illuminated by the sun is a beautiful golden orange, threaded with delicate ribbons of yellow. It sparkles dazzling the eyes.

Her face is soft and strong. A beautifully designed structure that has been covered by lovely velvety skin. Her cheekbone, for I can only see one from this side, is high and smoothly curved. The one eye that I can see is open and looking straight ahead. I have never been this close to her before. I have waited so long for this exact moment. The moment when finally, I would understand why she keeps showing up. What is it that connects us?

It was only after a minute of staring that I realized that her beautiful auburn hair was emerging out of the bottom of a leather aviator's helmet. The goggles had been lifted up, held tight against her forehead with the strap that went over her ear flaps and around her head. No one else could have looked so beautiful wearing that on their head.

Suddenly she turned to face me. My mind explodes with fire and energy as I see her full face and know that she sees mine. The explosion is so loud. It roars. It's not an explosion. It's an engine whining with a high pitch as it strains. We are in a small two-seater plane. We are flying. The engine cannot bear the load. I can smell smoke now and the pitch of the whining is increasing. It doesn't sound good.

"What are we going to do?" She says calmly, her first words to me, I wish I could have heard them better. "What are we going to do?" She repeats motioning her head forward with a nod.

I look ahead. We are only a few hundred feet from the treetops and descending at about a 45-degree angle. The plane can't carry the load of both of us. I know instantaneously that I will jump. I also know that she will be fine. I always know. I turn back to look over my left shoulder at her. She is still looking at me.

"I'm going to jump." I say matter-of-factly.

"I know," she says. "Thank you."

I reach down for the door latch and pull it up. The door cracks open just a little and I can hear the wind rushing by.

"Before I go, I have to ask you something."

She nods.

"Why don't you ever show up in my real life?"

Looking back at me with big sympathetic eyes she says, "I am your real life."

I shrug, open the door and roll out into the sky. As soon as my weight is released the engine stops whining so loudly. The plane starts to arc up and away from me as I fall.

"Who are you?" I shout, but it is too late.

...

Inside the plane she closes the door and pushes the latch down securely. She knew he wouldn't die, and she knew, that he knew, he wouldn't die, but she still admired him for jumping. It was still courageous and beautiful. He wasn't going to die, but it wouldn't be a pleasant landing either.

...

The air rushed past me on all sides as I watched the plane peel away. Suddenly I felt the topmost branches of the trees start to rip into my back. This wasn't going to be fun. A sharp pain in my left side, then another on my right. Little pricks all over. Then it was over.

...

I woke up with a convulsion as if I was hitting the ground. My heart was pounding from the excitement of the dream. It was another dream about the woman with the auburn hair. She was there. Right next to me. I spoke to her for the first time. The encounter couldn't have been more disappointingly brief, but still, it happened and if it happened once, it could happen again.

I picked up the notebook on the side of my bed and described the dream as best I could remember it. When I was done outlining the dream, I wrote the number 21 at the top of the page. It was the twenty-first time I had dreamed about her and it was the first time that we had ever spoken. I just wish it could have been longer. I didn't get her name.

Suddenly, I remembered the night before at the satsang

with Dr. Free and my clear decision to surrender my life to spiritual freedom. I had felt so strange the previous night, so otherworldly. Something had shifted, I know it did. I can't feel it the same way right now, but I know that the life I am living now is not the same as the one I was living yesterday morning. My karmic path has shifted. Nothing will ever be the same.

# CHAPTER FIVE

I met Dr. Free at satsang nearly thirty years ago, and nothing was ever the same, but let me tell you what I noticed this morning. I went back to the park to read. This time I was halfway through *Ubik* by Philip K. Dick. As you can guess, I was hoping to see one of my three lady friends with the suitcases, but none of them were there. So, I sat down to read. After a few minutes I heard the notification beep telling me that a text had arrived. I opened my phone and found that it was just a message telling me that something I had ordered was being delivered today. As I started to put the phone back into my pocket, I noticed a bright blue and green app icon on the screen. It was nestled between my iTunes app and Google Maps.

It was a beautiful app icon. It had a capital letter 'E' on it and the background looked like a spiral galaxy. It was not something I had downloaded, and I wondered how it had gotten on my phone. A few years ago, I had woken up with an album by the musical group U2 on my phone. I spent a few days trying to figure out where that had come from, before hearing in the news that the band had given copies of the album away to everyone who used iTunes and that the Apple company had delivered the albums overnight. I can see why the band members might have thought this was an act of tremendous generosity that would be welcomed by fans and newbies alike. What it actually stirred was a huge uproar. There wasn't an outcry of appreciation for the gifts, but rather cries of violation. People felt that their privacy had been violated. No one had wanted a demonstration that the Apple Corporation had complete access to their phone. If they could upload an album overnight, what else could they do? This act of generosity, which I realize was probably calculated to win new fans, backfired in a glorious way. Apologies occurred all around, and when I saw U2 live in concert over a year later they opened by thanking everyone for coming and apologizing again for the intrusion on everyone's privacy.

That story is what came to mind as I looked at the beautiful blue icon that had appeared on my phone overnight. Was Apple doing it again? Had they not learned their lesson the first time? Or was this some kind of spam, maybe even a virus that had been planted on my phone? Maybe if I open it, a destructive algorithm will infiltrate my phone. I decided to play it safe and just delete it. I pressed my finger over it waiting for it to shake to life so that it could be removed. All of the other icons started to shake, ready to be moved or deleted, but the 'E' icon stood still and unmovable. Oh shit, it was a hack. There was nothing I could do. I couldn't put it in the trash and erase it, and I didn't want to open it. I put the phone back in my pocket, deciding that I would look for more information about the icon when I was home. Certainly, I was not the only one who had ever encountered the mysterious 'E' app, and someone would surely know what it was and how to get rid of it.

I read for another hour or so and headed home. I was on the lookout the whole way for one of the three ladies –

for some reason I had become convinced that there were only three – but not one of them appeared anywhere along my route. I got home and onto my computer and started searching for information on the mysterious app. I started by searching for "E App." All I found were references to an entertainment app called 'E!'. So, I tried searching for "an app appeared on my phone last night" and I found out that this is a more common problem than I thought. It seems that many people experience all kinds of apps downloading automatically overnight, but no mention of anything like the one I was seeing. I kept hunting using different search variations, but eventually I gave up. There was nothing. I looked back at my phone and it was gone. No, not gone; it had moved. It was now sitting between my camera and my calendar. How strange an app that uploads itself and then moves around your screen on its own. I didn't have any more time to spend on the app mystery because I had to get back to work.

I am a teacher and a writer by the way, did I tell you that? I teach meditation and awakening and write spiritual books and novels. Everything that I create is designed to share some of the mystery that I have opened to over the years. It is a futile effort. I know. A mystery can never be shared in words. It can't be described or explained. Still, I hope that I can find the right words to point to all that heavenly glory. I believe that if people can avoid the temptation to worry too much about what I say and what they think I think it means, then the words can direct their attention and intention to something beyond the words. Well, at least that's the theory. Since the COVID-19 pandemic kicked into high gear I've been teaching exclusively online, which I really enjoy, and I've been working on a number of writing projects simultaneously. Today, I have to do some edits on a book about accessing higher states of consciousness, and if I have more time, I can continue writing my new novel.

After spending a few hours writing I had completely forgotten about the mysterious little app icon on my phone, but when I picked up the phone and saw the app, I nearly fell over. The blue/green app no longer had a letter 'E' on it. Instead it had a picture of the face of the girl with the auburn hair that I had seen in twenty-one of my dreams. As I looked closely at her image on the icon, my legs got weak. I started to rock on my heels, and I had to rest against the wall next to me not to fall over. How is this possible? How could her face appear on this icon? No one, literally no one but me, had ever seen her. Unless someone saw the sketches I drew of her in my dream notebook, but that's impossible. How did she get on my phone? All thoughts of viruses and destructive algorithms left me and I clicked on the icon. It expanded open.

In big bold letters it said:

### WELCOME TO e-Ternity
### the app beyond time.

Below that it said,

### ENTER YOUR PASSWORD

Password! What password? I didn't have a password. How could I have a password, I didn't even download this fucking app?

...

My body ached all over and was covered in little branches and leaves. I was flat on my back looking up through the trees. That had been a long fall. I saw a plume of smoke billowing upward in the sky and the little plane that I had just jumped out of, was spiraling toward the ground. "Oh no! She isn't going to make it." I thought as I jumped up and ran to a spot clear of trees so I could see better. From the clearing I could see the plane falling fast. After only a few moments it was lost behind the trees and suddenly I could hear a dull thudding sound followed by an explosion, a flash of light and more smoke rising into the sky.

I looked down toward the ground in sadness and I noticed my body was not aching at all anymore. This is a dream, I remembered. This isn't real. She didn't die, she isn't even real. I looked up into the sky and I saw a small figure tied to a parachute. It must be her. She was swaying back and forth slowly as she floated downward. She must be at least a mile away, but she was alive. She had gotten out of the plane in time. I started walking in the direction that she was falling, soon she was below the tree line. "How am I going to find her?" I thought. "It doesn't matter, I am going to find her, whatever it takes."

I started walking through the woods. It was a forest of trees, some pines and some that look like oaks and maybe maples. The sun shone through in patches through the canopy above. I had walked only about five minutes when I heard the sound of a human voice.

"Help." I heard a faint voice say. I looked around but I couldn't see anyone even though the voice sounded nearby. "Up here," the voice said.

It was her. Hanging from her parachute way up in the treetops. She was swaying from side to side a good sixty feet from the ground.

"I am so glad you're OK!" I shouted. It didn't occur to me to wonder how I could have found her this fast when she had looked at least a mile away just a few minutes ago, but it was definitely the woman with the auburn hair. She was still in her full aviator suit with her leather helmet still on her head and her goggles still strapped over her ears.

"How am I going to get down?" she asked.

"I don't know. Do you have a knife on you? Maybe you could cut yourself down."

"What? And just fall to the ground?"

"Yeah, that's probably not a great plan." I said stamping one foot on the ground to test how hard it was. Then something struck me. "Hey, this is a dream, right?"

"It is, yes." She said matter-of-factly.

"Then why don't you just fly down. You can do anything you want in a dream."

"You will have to fly up here and get me. It isn't my dream, it's yours. You can do whatever you want, but I can't. Not in your dream anyway. Not unless you give me permission."

"Ok, you have my permission."

"Dream manipulation is not that simple. Giving permission is complicated. It will be much easier for you to just fly up here and get me. You have to know, without any doubt, that you can do it," she explained. "Give it a try. It is just a dream. Of course, you can fly up here and get me." The logic seemed reasonable enough to me, so I just relaxed and imagined myself floating upward. Nothing.

"I can't do it." I said. "Nothing is happening."

"Ok, I will have to do it the hard way." She took out a knife and cut one of the cords that tethered her to the parachute that was dangling from the trees. The cord snapped and she fell down a few feet with a gasp and a jerk. "Ok, one down, five to go." She went ahead cutting through each cord one at a time, and each time she fell a little further. When there was one cord left, she was about twenty feet from the ground. She cut it and fell. She hit the ground and gracefully rolled forward over her shoulder and landed in a standing position. "Ok!" she said, "That wasn't so bad."

"Sorry I couldn't help," I said limply.

"You really couldn't do it?" She asked.

"Nope."

"OK, try this. It's the simplest trick in the book. First let me turn around. Now, imagine there is something, maybe a glass of water, sitting on the ground behind you. Picture it in your mind in detail. Then turn around and see if it is there."

I did as she said and turned around. Nothing. "Nope, nothing. Didn't work."

She walked toward me. "Well, that's odd. Maybe this isn't your dream either."

"What do you mean, it's not my dream? Whose dream is it?" I demanded.

"I don't know." Then she seemed to realize something and added. "Oh yeah, where you come from everyone still assumes that every dream they have at night belongs to them. The fact is, there are lots of dreams out there and it is actually rare to end up in one of your own."

Just then it dawned on me that we were together. I

was finally with the girl with the auburn hair. I had been dreaming about her for five years and here she was standing in front of me.

"You've been dreaming with me for a lot longer than five years," she said with a compassionate look on her beautiful face.

"How did you know what I was thinking?" I asked with all the indignation I could muster, as if I had been violated and really cared, but I really didn't. I was too happy just being here with her. I couldn't have cared less that she could read my mind.

"I can do that sometimes. Not always. You can think about it as a good guess if you like. It is more or less like that anyway."

Once again, I stepped into the present moment and realized who I was with. Holding out my hand I said, "I'm Brian." She took my hand and hers felt so lovely in my hand - soft and smooth, but also strong and confident.

"My name is Innocence," she told me.

"That's a beautiful name," I responded.

"Thanks."

"So, you know that I have been dreaming about you for a long time. Do you know why?" I asked.

"I don't know why, but I know I'm here to find out."

"This is still a dream, right?" I asked, starting to realize that I didn't know what was going on.

"Yes, it is still a dream. But the life you were in when you went to sleep before you woke up in this dream, was also a dream. But listen, there are too many questions and I can't answer them all right now in the first few minutes. Let me just say very briefly that you are being awoken into the dreamscape." I started to protest, and she put her finger on my lips to quiet me. My whole body shuddered to feel her finger touch my lip. "Don't ask questions. Answers will come. Just accept this for the moment. There are many dimensions to reality. More than anyone knows, and new ones being added constantly. What you call dreams, which by the way is everything you know, are thresholds that exist between dreams. Dreams are the trans-dimensional space that other dimensions float in. Each dimension is a being, an energetic form of intelligence. Each is a god of one or more dream realms. The life you live as Brian was your first dream, it will always feel uniquely real because it was the first. This is another dream. You've been here many times before."

"OK." I said obstinately, "Can we slow down?"

"No. We don't have time to waste, and besides this will all go a lot easier for both of us if you just trust me."

I turned away and closed my eyes. I bit down hard on my tongue to try to wake myself up from this dream.

"That never works," she said as she walked around to face me again. "Sit down," as she gestured toward a fallen tree that offered us enough space to sit together. I sat and she sat down next to me. "I am going to try to explain to you what is going on. What I am about to tell you is all true, but I have to speak in vague terms for now. Please listen and trust me. Ok, here we go. I am a very important person in the dreamscape and someone or something is trying to kill me. To be fair, they might not even know they are doing it, but still they are. I was given permission to awaken you to help me."

"Why me?" I interrupted.

"Don't interrupt. I am giving you information in the best way that I can. But to satisfy your curiosity, let's just say that you were in the right place at the right time and you had the raw talent I needed. I first connected with you in your DreamOne, that's the one that feels like reality to you, when you were about two years old. We met often for a couple of years and then I had to stop. Anyway, the seeds were planted, and they came to fruition just as they were supposed to. You remember the experience of cosmic consciousness you had in July of 2001?"

"Yes."

"That was the fruition. All of this," she waved her arms around, "could have happened any time after that, but I've been waiting for the right moment. I saw the moment coming about five years ago in your DreamOne time and that's when I started contacting you again in the dreamscape."

This all sounded reasonable in a dream-logic sort of way. I sat for a minute in silence trying to weigh my options. Most likely this was just a dream, like any other dream, and soon I would wake up and realize it. Then I would write all these details down and this would be my twenty-second dream with the girl with the auburn hair. If that was the case I might as well just go along with all this. It is just a dream anyway. Why fight it? I can just accept whatever she says and keep doing it. I had done some improv theater at one time and this would be just like that. I would just approach everything with the yes attitude of improv. But what if this wasn't a simple dream in the ordinary sense. What if she was telling me the truth and I really was waking up to a wider reality that occurs within dreams? What if there really are higher dimensional beings and I really am floating in the space between them? If that were true, then I really had no choice but to go along with what she said. So, either way, the outcome was the same. Just go along with whatever she says and see what happens.

"So, what now?" I said. She smiled and nodded affectionately, and to be honest that is probably all she needed to do in order to keep me in line.

In a more serious tone she said, "Something has been released into your DreamOne world that is a threat to me and we have to find out what it is and figure out how to get rid of it."

I pulled my phone out of my pocket and tapped the screen to life. "I think I've already found it," I said, and I pointed to the e-Ternity app on the screen. It took me a minute to find it because it had moved to the second page now. Her face was still on the icon.

She snatched the phone out of my hand. "Where'd you get that?" she demanded.

"I don't know. It just appeared there overnight."

"Open it for me," she said, and I tapped on the icon and it opened. "What's the password?" she asked.

"That's the thing, I don't know."

She looked up into the air as if she was thinking. "Yeah, this is definitely it. Have you seen any unusual people in DreamOne recently? Maybe three women?"

I told her the whole story about the three women with the flower print suitcase. She listened attentively until the end.

"Yes, that's them," she said. Then she started looking all around as if something was happening.

"We only have a moment. Listen, you have to find

those women. You have to get all three of them together and find out what they know about this app. You got it?"

...

Suddenly I was opening my eyes in bed. It was morning and I had just had an amazing dream about the woman with the auburn hair. I reached down for my notebook and described every detail that I could remember.

# CHAPTER SIX

I am very still in the water, looking at the zendo on the shore. The Roshi with the long white beard is inside now. I get even more still. The surface of the water is just above the bridge of my nose. I can't see even a ripple. I am not moving at all. I can't even tell if I am separate from the water. I am not moving and so I can't tell if I exist at all. That's how it works. Perfect stillness is non-existence. There is nothing for me to do here right now except wait, as patiently as I can. This is definitely where it is going to happen. I'm early. So, all I have to do is wait.

...

My life was never the same after that first encounter with Dr. Free, and the next year was a tough one. It also seems to have set a pattern that has repeated itself in my life over and over again. First there is an initial spiritual opening. That leads to a turbulent time that is perhaps a necessary integration of whatever was realized. Finally, there is some dramatic second experience that seems to be the culmination of the original one. Well, that is certainly what happened during the year after I encountered Dr. Free.

I was married when I met Dr. Free. Rochelle was a lovely woman and we had been together for about five years. She was, in fact, the one who introduced me to spiritual life in the first place. She loved the Harvard psychedelic professor-turned-guru Ram Dass. She gave me his book *Grist for the Mill* a few weeks after we had met. And a few months later we went to see the now beardless Western Guru when he spoke in Cambridge. I loved reading *Grist for the Mill* and I loved seeing Ram Dass speak live that night in Cambridge.

At the time, I was working as an associate engineer in a small high-tech company called Lasertronics. We made semiconductor laser diodes for the then booming telecommunications industry. I worked in the research and development department. My bosses all had PhDs from MIT. They would design new laser products and I would fabricate prototypes in the lab. It was good work and perhaps the best thing about it was that it provided me with the time and money I needed to explore things that interested me.

Ram Dass' *Grist for the Mill* wasn't the first spiritual book Rochelle had given to me. Only days after we met she gifted me with a copy of her favorite book, *Illusions: The Adventures of a Reluctant Messiah* by Richard Bach. When I read *Illusions,* I had never read a "new age" spiritual book before. I was totally hooked. The book was filled with pithy short quotes that revealed a new world of understanding to me.

I was raised Catholic. My parents were second generation Americans and my grandparents were all Portuguese, and three of them had been born in the Azores - a small group of Portuguese-controlled islands located far off the coast in the Atlantic Ocean. When I was very young, I had wanted to be a priest. One day I mustered up the courage to talk to my grandfather about it. I couldn't have been more than four or five years old. My grandfather seemed to be the most important person in the family, so he was a natural person to talk to about the sacred calling I was feeling. I approached him as he sat in his rocker chewing on the stub of a lit cigar.

"Grampa, I want to be a priest." I said expectantly.

"Good idea." He said in return and then rubbing the forefingers and thumb of his right hand together he added, "Good racket! You see that Lincoln they drive?" He was referring to their car, owned by the church of course. My heart sank. I had no idea that people became priests for the money. I no longer had any interest in the priesthood. I soon decided that I wanted to be a scientist and after a few years I declared, to my father this time, that I was an atheist. Every Sunday when I refused to go to church, we had a long conversation about how important it was to believe in something.

"I don't care if you don't believe in God," he would say, "but you have to believe in something."

"I believe in science," I would invariably declare, and a discussion would ensue. There was never a clear winner to the debate, but in the end, I generally didn't go to church either. Of course, today I teach meditation and have lived the lion's share of my adult life devoted to spiritual fulfillment, so my father seems to have been the clear winner.

Rochelle introducing me to Richard Bach and Richard Alpert, *aka* Ram Dass, had knocked me squarely onto the spiritual path. I had been doing some meditation already, but strictly in a secular psychological context. Now, I was interested in enlightenment. I wanted to see through the limitations of my small self-identity and realize the true source of universal consciousness. As my spiritual destiny unfolded it brought Dr. Free's book into my life and then orchestrated my dramatic encounter with the man himself.

I only remembered the initial frozen-time episode with Dr. Free a few weeks after it happened. The very next day I only remembered him finishing talking with me and moving on to someone else. The next thing I knew, I was waking up from a dream about the auburn-haired lady. A week or so later I started to remember everything that had happened after time stopped, but I never told anyone about it; in fact, it was a number of years before I even asked Dr. Free about it. When I described my experience of that night to him all he said was, "Yes, awakening can get pretty weird." It was clear he didn't want to go into it anymore and so I let it go.

A few days after my mind had been blown in satsang, I got a call from a lady named Jessie. She was a close student of Dr. Free's who was then living in Dr. Free's community in Marin County California; but she was originally from Boston and was the main organizer of Dr. Free's satsangs there. It seemed that his satsangs had stirred up the interest of a small group of people and Jessie was calling to see if I would like to be part of a local study group. I said yes, and she gave me the phone number of a man named Sean Forester who was forming the group with his wife Olivia.

After hanging up the phone I sat down. I was excited to pursue my involvement with other people who were interested in Dr. Free's teaching work, but I was also worried about Rochelle. I could easily see myself getting very involved with this work and I instinctively knew that it would lead to turbulence in our relationship. I decided that I could do both. I could pursue this spiritual path and build my life with Rochelle at the same time.

Going to the first meeting at Sean and Olivia's was thrilling and anxiety provoking. Afterall, I didn't know either of them at all. Presumably they had been at the satsang gatherings with me, but there were at least eighty people there, so it was likely that I never met them. They lived in a small but well-kept house in Newton, a fairly affluent town just west of Boston. I arrived early as I always did and parked my light blue Honda Civic a few blocks away to wait until 7:00pm when the meeting was scheduled to start.

I sat for a few minutes and then I saw someone park just a few spaces down from me. The car door opened, and I saw Bob get out. I was so excited to see someone familiar that I opened my door and shouted out to him, "Bob!" as if we were the best of friends. He turned when he heard his name and recognizing me, he smiled big and wide. It seemed that he was happy to see a familiar face, too.

"Hi, Brian. You comin' to this shindig tonight?"

"Yes, you too?"

"I'm here just for that."

"Do you know Sean and Olivia?" I asked.

"Nope. But I've been working with Dr. Free for about five years and he suggested that the group might benefit from my involvement, so here I am." Then he added as if just remembering, "I looked for you after that last satsang, but you were gone. It looked like you got your brain melted by Dr. Free. I was a little worried about you driving home."

"I'll be honest with you, Bob, I don't remember driving

home. I just woke up the next morning still rocked from what Dr. Free had said the night before."

"Yeah, I'm not surprised. OK, let's head in, don't want to keep everyone waiting."

The apartment was clean and simple with a lot of Zen-looking art and sculptures around. I didn't recognize either Sean or Olivia from the satsang, but they seemed like good people. He was a psychologist and she was a fundraiser for a non-profit. Sean wore wire framed glasses and had the air of an intellectual. Olivia might have passed for a stereotypical suburban housewife except for a long stream of bright purple colored hair that hung down the left side of her face. She greeted me as I walked in with a quick handshake followed by what felt like an extra-long hug. Sean did exactly the same, and I realized it was just the way they greeted guests.

Aside from Bob and I, there were two other people at that first meeting. Arav Patel was from India. He had just finished his PhD in computer science at Boston University and was seeking enlightenment. Then there was Joice Richards. She was a nurse in one of the big Boston hospitals. She had a background in the theosophical writings of Alice Bailey and had been hoping to find a study group like this for years.

That meeting was very simple. We each introduced ourselves to the group and spoke about what we were hoping to get out of our meetings. It seemed that we were all on the same page, wanting to gain a better understanding of Dr. Free's teachings and have a group to do spiritual practice together with. Bob's story was the most interesting.

Bob was retired from military intelligence. He had

been an electrical engineer specializing in communications technology. "I did 'spy stuff' for the military," he said with a wink. Now that he was retired, he had turned his attention over to the quest for enlightenment and the development of technologies that would help people awaken to their true nature. He had brought a CD to show us. He explained that the CD had been altered to contain bilateral beats that would harmonize the left and right hemispheres of the brain and trigger enlightenment. The CD he brought contained one of my favorite albums, Pink Floyd's *Wish You Were Here*, now digitally enhanced with bilateral beats to blow your mind. He was starting a business to manufacture these. He gave one to each of us and explained that we should listen to the CD played at a loud volume and using headphones. I was very intrigued.

There was no way to know it at the time, but twenty years later, as Dr. Free's spiritual community was collapsing under the weight of his own many shortcomings, only Bob and I would still be around from that original group. Over the next year, however, we met faithfully every Tuesday night from 7:00 until about 9:30pm. After meditating, we would read a passage from Dr. Free's book and discuss it. On the first Thursday of every month we would watch a ninety-minute video recording of one of Dr. Free's recent satsangs from around the world. By the end of the year, two other women had become regular members of the group. Darleen and Clarise. They were a couple both in their thirties and deeply in love. Arav and I were the youngest members of the group both in our late twenties.

That was an exciting year. I learned so much every time we met, not only about what Dr. Free taught, but also about the dynamics of a group discussion. Generally, it was cordial, but occasionally Joice would get angry and curse about something she didn't understand or agree with. The group didn't all stay together through that first year. The first to leave was Olivia. A few months after the group got started a young graduate student named Marco joined. He had seen Dr. Free in Scandinavia where he had just moved from to study at Harvard. A few weeks after he started in the group, he announced that he was leaving his graduate studies to move into Dr. Free's community in California. We were all so excited for him, or at least I thought we all were. We congratulated him and offered to help in any way that we could. He left the meeting a little early that night and after he was gone Olivia let us know how she really felt.

"Do you guys really think this is a good idea? He's about to throw his graduate opportunity away, for what? To join Dr. Free's community. What good is that going to do him. I don't understand how you can support this. He is young and bright. He has an amazing life ahead of him. A graduate degree from Harvard will give him so much. And it was a full scholarship. I don't understand how you can all just support this crazy idea." Once she was done, she got up and walked out of the room.

We all just sat there. I was completely surprised. We had all spent the last few months talking about leaving the world behind and embracing the possibility of enlightenment. We talked about the current state of the world and why spiritual upliftment was really what the world needed now more than anything. Olivia seemed to be one of the loudest voices in favor of leaving the world behind. That was the last meeting Olivia attended and Sean announced that he was leaving the group a few weeks later. The rest of us started meeting at Darleen and Clarise's apartment in Jamaica Plains on Tuesdays and we rented a room in a spiritual bookstore in Cambridge for our monthly videos.

I would occasionally invite the whole group to my place for dinner. Rochelle and I would cook, and she really liked everyone. She would always participate in the conversation, but she never wanted to get any further involved with the group. At the same time, I was spending more and more time doing meditation practice and spending time with the other group members. Arav and I got close. Mostly we went out for coffee to talk about enlightenment and spiritual practice. Things started to get more and more tense between Rochelle and me. It was obvious to both of us that we were growing apart. I kept trying to invite her to activities with the group, and she kept inviting me to spend time with her, but it was clearly not working. At some point I realized that we were not going to stay together. We might not split up today, it might be next year, or a few years down the line, but it was clear that we were not destined to spend our entire lives together. I also knew that the longer we did stay together the harder it would be for both of us.

One day it was finally clear. We needed to split up and I needed to be the one to initiate it. It didn't have to do with not loving her, I still did, and I knew that she still loved me, but we were not living the same lives anymore. She wanted a more conventional life and I wanted a spiritual life. It is funny, we had shared a dream of living a spiritual life together, but once I got deeply involved with Dr. Free's community, she started wanting children. I didn't want to hold her back from having the life she wanted, and I didn't want to sacrifice the life I wanted. Most of all, I didn't want us to end up in a life of compromise in which neither of us were happy, and we both resented the other. So, one night I asked her if we could talk. I think she already guessed what was coming. I had been obsessing over it all day. I was terrified. I had never done anything like this before. I had never before stepped so far out of the status quo. In my upbringing, divorce was unthinkable. My aunt had gotten divorced and we didn't speak to her for five years, and she only lived a half mile away. I was ready to lose my whole family if need be. I was determined to live a life devoted to spirit and nothing was going to stop me.

Rochelle sat down calmly. I got ready to speak and suddenly I heard a deafening scream inside my head. It was as if someone was screaming "No!" as loudly as they could in both of my ears. It was terrifying. The sound actually hurt. "Noooooooooo!" it said. I opened my mouth and I said, "Rochelle, I don't think we can stay married any longer." As the words came out of my mouth, I could not hear them because the scream in my ears was too loud. I felt my mouth move and the air pass over my lips and tongue, so I knew that I had said them, but I couldn't hear a thing. Once the words were out everything went perfectly silent.

Suddenly, I felt weightless. I actually felt as if I was floating off the seat I was sitting on. This was such a physical feeling that I swept my right hand under the seat and expected there to be a two- or three-inch gap separating me from the seat cushion. There wasn't. I was firmly planted on the chair, but I felt like I was floating in midair. I felt free. It was as if I had been wearing a straitjacket made of lead. It had been put on me at birth, or soon after, and it was heavy. It kept me wrapped up tight and weighed me down. It was made up of all of my ideas about what I should do, and shouldn't do, what was right and what was wrong, what was good and what was bad. All of those ideas had been wrapped around me layer upon layer and suddenly they had all fallen off. I felt as light as a feather. Suddenly, everything was possible. I didn't know what I should or shouldn't do anymore. Can you imagine how it would feel to have a lead straitjacket that you had been wearing your entire life finally removed? I suddenly knew that this, this lightness of being, THIS, was what life really felt like! Life felt good! Life was alive! Life was happy and free and wild. Life was love of life. I was laughing so hard. I was so happy. Rochelle was still sitting in front of me. I was barely aware of her at this moment. I wonder what I must have looked like.

Then suddenly, I started to cry. I thought about all of the millions and millions of people all over the world dragging through life wearing leaden straitjackets. They had no idea how happy it felt to be alive, just like I had had no idea just a few minutes ago. I thought about how heavy and burdened everyone felt and I was so sad. I cried so hard. My belly hurt from crying. I remembered that this was how I had cried when I was a baby. I would cry with my whole body, in huge convulsive heaves. Tears were streaming down my cheeks and I was so sad.

Then I remembered how quickly my lead suit had come off and the idea that everyone could just flick their straightjackets off in a second struck me as a cosmic joke. We were all so burdened by something we could remove in a second. It was so funny. I started laughing again, laughing just as hard as I had cried. Laughing with my whole body. Convulsing until my belly hurt in a different way. The pain was so bad from laughing that I couldn't continue. And I realized again how much everyone was suffering and I cried hard again until my belly ached in the first way. I cycled back and forth through fits of crying and laughing for ten or twelve cycles. It must have been twenty or thirty minutes. When it was done, I was absolutely exhausted. I looked up, my face full of tears and snot. Rochelle was just looking at me. We didn't say any more that night. I slept downstairs on the couch. We never slept in the same bed again after that.

# CHAPTER SEVEN

It had been a few weeks since I had announced to Rochelle that our marriage needed to end that Dr. Free arrived in Boston for another round of satsangs. I had asked if I could meet with him and he told me to wait for him after the first night's satsang. Dr. Free had a small private room where he met with people when satsang was done. Bob found me soon after satsang had ended to tell me that Dr. Free was ready to see me. I walked with Bob to the door of the private room in the back of the same yoga studio where I had attended my first satsang.

"What have you done?" Dr. Free said with a smile as I walked in the door.

"I broke up with Rochelle," I said and he smiled wider.

"Do you see now why for millennia monks would go off to live in monasteries?"

"Yes, I think I do. I feel so free. I also feel very guilty. I broke a big promise and Rochelle did not deserve that," I said with a tear of grief running down my face.

"How is she?"

"It hurts." I admitted honestly. "But she is amazingly understanding. She said to me that if I was leaving for a Las Vegas showgirl, she would have been pissed; but since I am leaving for God, what can she do?" Then I added, "You know the neighbors came up with a plan. They wanted to ambush me after work one night and yell at me until I stopped doing what I was doing. They wanted to save me from your cult, I think." I said with a chuckle, but then wondered if I had gone too far. Dr. Free laughed out loud and I was relieved. "She told them to go to hell," I concluded.

"You are a lucky man. It must say something good about you that you chose such an openhearted wife," he said. And in my head, I wondered, "Yes, but what does it say about me that I left her?"

"You know, ever since I told her, I feel like I'm floating in mid-air. It is as if a huge weight got lifted off my body and now, I am free floating through life. And a few days after Rochelle and I talked, I woke up with a big round hole in my chest. It feels like the skin has been peeled off and all of my nerve endings are exposed. I feel everything. I feel what other people are feeling, sometimes I even see their thoughts form into words in their mouths just before they speak." I was very excited now, speaking faster and faster.

"Yes, you are opening up to higher dimensions of reality. It won't stop you know. The opening keeps getting wider and wider as long as you don't close down to it. My job is to help you stay open and, if I have to, force you to stay open. If," he paused, "that is the role you want me to play in your life. Do you want me to take you on as my student?"

"Yes, Dr. Free, I want you to be my teacher."

"Are you sure?"

"Yes, I am absolutely sure. All of this happened because of you."

"Ok then, you're in." Then he turned toward Bob and said, "Hey Bob, Brian can stay with you at your place. It's big enough, don't you think?"

Bob looked startled for a moment and glanced at the half dozen or so other people in the room, almost as if he was looking for someone to come to his rescue. "Ah, yes that's a great idea!" he said with exaggerated enthusiasm.

"Wonderful idea," Dr. Free responded.

I waited that night until Dr. Free was finished seeing people and I walked up to Bob as he left the yoga studio. "Hey Bob, do you really think it's a good idea for me to move in with you?"

"Yeah, sure. You need a place to stay and I need company. We can get you moved in any day this week, or as soon as you are ready. You won't be able to bring too much stuff; my place isn't really all that big."

"I won't have much anyway," I said honestly. "And thanks a lot. It really is going to help me."

I wasn't ready to move for another week, but by the next Saturday I was packed up and driving off from what was now Rochelle's house. I had left her with the house, one of the cars and all the furniture. I was leaving with my Honda Civic, $2000 cash, my apple IIE computer, and three trash bags full of clothes in the backseat. That week was actually wonderful. Something dropped between Rochelle and I and it was like meeting again for the first time. Suddenly all of the pressure of trying to navigate our life together was gone and we could just be ourselves again. It was amazing to see how much we had each changed to accommodate the other. It had taken time, and it wasn't noticeable while it was happening, but now it was so clear that we had each let go of so much in order to be together. Ironically, it was during this last week of us living together that I realized how much I really did love Rochelle.

Rochelle was waving from our front door as I drove off.
I remember her standing looking a little lost. I felt terrible
as I drove away. I knew that I had ruined all of our plans
and aspirations together. I also knew that it was something
that I had to do, and that we would both be better off
for it in the long run. That was what I believed anyway. I
have thought about my decision to leave her many times.
I was leaving a wonderful woman, and a very good life in
every conventional sense, to join a spiritual community
that almost anyone would see as a cult. It was the first truly
unprecedented decision I had ever made. Nothing had prepared me for it. I can only attribute it to the strength of the
experience that I was still having as I drove off. Even then,
in the midst of the sadness and grief, I still felt as if there
was a large round whole exposing my chest cavity and the
beating heart that lay within it. It was as if my emotional
sensitivity was dialed all the way up. It was very intense and
yet it still felt totally right.

Bob lived in a condo on Beacon Hill in Boston. The
building had once been a large stone church that was now
renovated into four unique apartments. Bob's was on the
second floor. I rang the bell at the street level entrance and
heard Bob's voice.

"Yep."

"It's Brian." Then I heard the buzzing that meant the
door was open. I pushed on it then walked in and up the
stairs.

Bob let me in through the door to his apartment. I had
been in it once before but only briefly.

"Not much to show you. Here is the living room," he
said gesturing around the room we had just walked into.

"And that is my bedroom," he said pointing to a door to the left of the entrance. "The bathroom, and your room. You will see that it still has some stuff in it, but I think it will work for you."

I walked into the room that he had indicated was mine. "It's great," I said. And it really was. A small room with a stone wall and a big stained-glass window. It had a double bed in it and a workbench. On the bench there were all kinds of electronics. "What's all that?" I asked, pointing to the workbench.

"That's where I create things. I didn't know where to move it to, so I just left it for now. I will tell you all about it later. We should run down and get your stuff before you get a ticket."

It only took about an hour to get my stuff up into the apartment, but it took nearly twice that long to find a parking space for the night. Parking was going to be an issue, but it always was in Boston. I walked through the door of the apartment with the key Bob had lent me.

"I'll get you your own key tomorrow," he offered.

"Thanks."

"I ordered some Chinese food from around the corner. It's a good place." He gestured toward the back of the living room where there was a kitchen area with a small table. The food had all been laid out there for us.

"Wow, thanks a lot, Bob. I feel I should have gotten you dinner. I really appreciate being able to stay here."

"No worries." said Bob casually. "Like Dr. Free said, it was a wonderful idea. I think it is going to be good for both of us."

We sat down and ate for a few minutes without talking.

Then Bob mentioned the electronic equipment in the next room.

"I guess in my retirement I've become a bit of an inventor. I told you that I had worked in army intelligence, right?"

"Yeah."

"I was part of the remote viewing experiments."

"Really?"

"Yeah, and I was the head of a team that was trying to take what we were learning about remote viewing and create a technology that would support it. They discovered early on that remote viewing was possible and that some people seemed to be naturally really good at it. When we found someone who was gifted, we would study them while they viewed. We would map their brain during the viewing. We wanted to create a helmet that would stimulate the same brain activity that we observed in people while they were viewing." Bob was obviously very excited about this work. He had lost all interest in his Chinese food and was waving his chopsticks around as he spoke. "That's where I first learned about bilateral beats. We were experimenting with those, too. And light pulses in the eyes. We made dozens of test helmets, some with headphones and eye goggles. They were of limited success. You know why?" He asked and then looked over at me.

"No," I said meekly.

"Because the biggest hurdle that a person needs to leap over is psychological. What makes it so hard for people to view remotely is that they don't believe it's possible. I think most of the success we had with the helmets came from the fact that people thought it was the helmet doing it. It was more of placebo technology than anything else. After I got involved in spiritual work, I realized that enlightenment is the same thing. The big obstacle is that people don't believe it's possible. Sure, maybe it's possible for some big guru or holy person, but not for me, right?" He paused but not long enough for a response. "So, over the last few years I started experimenting with some of the same technology I used years ago to see if I could create technologies that would stimulate enlightenment. And you know what? I have."

"Really, you mean like the CD's you gave all of us at the meeting?"

"That one was kid stuff. Purely entertainment really. But in the other room I have one that will knock your socks off." He looked down at the table and said, "Let's get this shit cleaned up and I'll show you."

We worked together and cleaned everything up. Then Bob had me sit down on the couch in the center of the living room. It was a really beautiful apartment. The walls were nearly covered from floor to ceiling with paintings and original artworks. Some nudes and some landscapes. All very beautiful, most fairly big.

"Bob, are you an artist?" I asked nodding toward the paintings on the wall.

"I don't paint or anything. I collect. I look for stuff that has feeling and spirit. I am pretty amateur, but I like it."

Bob had two sets of headphones in his hands and he was obviously much more interested in what he was about to show me than in anything that had to do with the art on the wall. He walked over to me and handed me one set. I put them on, there was complete silence.

"OK, you ready?" I heard Bob's voice say through the headphones.

"Hey, how come I can hear you through the headphones."

"I made 'em that way. Are you ready?"

"I'm ready when you are," I said.

"OK, this is the deluxe version of *Shine on You Crazy Diamond.*"

Then I heard the familiar spacey intro to the Pink Floyd song. Long notes that sounded like electronic horns strewn over with sprinkles of tinker bells that run down the sides of the chords. I opened my eyes and saw Bob sitting across from me with his headphones on. He motioned with his fingers for me to close my eyes, so I did. And I relaxed into the sound. The guitar started playing. It sounded so good, almost too good. The notes sounded like living beings. I could almost feel them running through my head and down my neck and all over my body. The edges of the hole in my chest started to vibrate. I started to shiver and just then the drums crashed through me. I wasn't in the room anymore. I was floating out in space. There were stars all around me. And there was Bob, just a few feet away. I heard Bob's voice in my head.

"Don't talk. Think it to me."

"Bob, the music is so beautiful. It is turning my insides out. It feels amazing," I thought.

"Keep relaxing. Let the sound take you. You are taking to this very well," Bob thought back.

The sound of the electric guitars seemed to propel me even faster through space. Each note was like an ocean wave that I was riding. I could see each note ripple through space, stars rising up as the note passed by and then falling back into place.

The first vocals of the song rang out, "Remember when you were young. You shone like the sun." As I heard these words, I started to remember something. Something that happened a long time ago, when I was very young. It was a journey that I had taken, or one that I remembered. It was important. The stars all around me were spinning very fast now. I was tumbling downward. Faster and faster I fell. Then more lyrics, "You reached for the secret too soon. You tried for the moon." Yes! I remember. I tried to bring it all with me. I tried to hold onto it all. I didn't want to let go. The hole in my chest, the one that I started feeling soon after breaking up with Rochelle, was burning now. The hole was all that was left of me. There was just a black hole in space. "Like black holes in the sky." Just like the song says.

"Bob, what's happening? I'm disappearing. There won't be anything left. I didn't mean to bring it all with me. I didn't know any better!" I was screaming loudly.

The music went silent and I heard Bob's voice from the room this time, not through the headphones. "You OK? Breathe Brian. Big deep breaths." I felt Bob's hand on my back. I had a back. My body was back. The hole in my chest was not burning now either.

"Jesus fucking Christ, Bob! What the hell was that?" I wasn't exactly angry, but I did feel like Bob hadn't been upfront with me about what this journey was going to be like.

"I am really sorry. I had no idea you were going to open up like that. It's never happened that way before. What was going on with you? Are you sure you're alright now? Here, have a glass of water." Bob handed me a tall glass of water and I drank it down quickly, some dribbled down my chin.

"Thanks," I said, much calmer now. Besides the fact that I was wet with sweat, I actually felt fine. "I'm not sure what happened. I can't remember it all. It feels like a dream. I know it had something to do with me being a small boy, but I don't know what it was. It felt like I tried to steal something, but I couldn't tell what." I noticed the headphones in my lap, and I picked them up. "What exactly are these supposed to do?"

"They use a very advanced version of the bilateral beat technology, or at least a very close cousin of that. I was working on it in the remote viewing lab just before we were shut down. I took a copy of the notes with me and, like I said, I have been repurposing the technology for spiritual awakening. I've had dozens of people listen to that same song on those headphones and nothing at all like this has ever happened before."

"But how does it work?"

"To make it simple let's say that it increases the vibration of your brainwaves. That was the most exciting part of the research we were doing with remote viewing. Your brain is like a receiver and it vibrates with energy entering into it from the cosmos. Higher frequency cosmic energy holds more information, but your brain has to be vibrating at high frequency to be able to receive that information. Normally our brains operate at a lower frequency, like this." Bob starts waving his hand in front of his face from left to right and back again, very slowly. When he starts speaking again, he only says one syllable at a time and only when his hand passes directly in front of his mouth. "At...

this...speed...you...can't...get...much...in...for...ma...tion."
He then starts moving his hand faster and speaking faster
to match it. "If we speed up the frequency much more information can come through." He said this last sentence so
fast there were no spaces between words.

"I see. But what kind of information was I getting? It
was all so jumbled and weird," I asked.

"Like I said, I've never seen anything like that before
at that frequency. I had the thing turned way down. I've
been wearing those things nearly every day for ten years. I
started at the frequency we just used and every six months
or so I raised the frequency slightly. I now listen regularly
at ten times that speed. You see, there is another factor to
be considered. It is not just the rate of speed that our brains
can take in information that matters, but also the capacity
of our minds to interpret that data. Initially your brain can't
make heads or tails out of the new high-speed data stream.
It starts making up stuff that feels like nonsense. It takes
a long time for the brain to make sense out of anything.
Once some meaning-making capacity has been built at a
certain frequency then you can go to a slightly higher one
and stabilize meaning-making there. That's how I ratcheted
up my own consciousness. If you want to, I can work with
you to ratchet up yours."

"After what I just experienced, I'm not sure I want that,
but maybe. What does Dr. Free think about all this?"

"He loves it. I made a set for him. He wears them all
the time at nearly full frequency and just says it feels pleasant. That guy's a freak, but that's why we love 'em. Anyway,
this all opens up into some pretty fascinating philosophical territory like, what is the mind? That's a fucker. You

can electronically stimulate the brain into high frequency operation, but the mind, which is the meaning-making mechanism, has to catch up. I write about the difference in my papers and sales literature."

I stopped him there. "You sell this shit?" I said.

"Well not yet, but someday."

Out of nowhere the sound of a high-pitched voice cried out. "Bob, you're beautiful! Bob, you're beautiful!"

"You haven't met Clarisse, yet. I'll go get her and introduce you two." Bob said as he walked to the bedroom. He returned in a moment with a huge bird cage covered in a bright purple cloth. From beneath the cloth the screeching voice said again, "Bob you're beautiful!" Bob pulled the cloth off the top of the cage to reveal a stunning white Cockatoo.

"Brian, this is Clarisse. Clarisse, this is Brian."

"Hello, Briaaaan," the beautiful bird screeched.

"Hi, Clarisse," I answered. "You're beautiful."

"Thank you," said Clarisse.

"You look better now," Bob said looking at me. "And you look tired, too. I think we should just get some sleep and talk about it more in the morning." I agreed and headed for my bedroom. I had had enough for one night.

# CHAPTER EIGHT

The last thing I remembered from the dream was that Innocence had told me that I had to find those three women. But how was I going to do that? Supposedly I have to find out what they know about the app. But this is all crazy. I am acting as if a dream is giving me instructions. It was just a dream after all. That girl with the auburn hair, Innocence, isn't a real person. It was just a dream. I got up and got dressed. I just need to get some work done and forget about that dream. I have a program to plan for and a book to write. I don't have time for nonsense.

I made an espresso in my favorite cup decorated with blue tile, like a Lisbon house. I sat at the table and sipped slowly looking out the window. Bob Johnson, my old friend from the Dr. Free days, was on my mind. If he were here, I am sure he would have an opinion about this. If he were around, we'd talk all night about it, probably come to nothing in the end, but we'd have fun doing it. I wonder if he's still in LA. Maybe I should see if I can find him online and give him a buzz. He'd love all this shit. Yup, I'll look him up online, see where he is, and call him tonight.

As that plan of action got clear my phone buzzed with an incoming text. "Hey buddy, it's Bob, I need to talk to you, can I call you tonight?" OK, that's weird, but that is the kind of connection Bob and I always had. I hadn't talked to him in a good 10 years. Amazing that the psychic hotline is still in operation. I would be more freaked out by the synchronicity of my deciding to call Bob at exactly the same moment that he texted me, except that kind of stuff used to happen to us all the time. I texted back "OK" and left it at that.

I'm feeling inspired so I decide to run out to the park and start with some reading. I have a new book from a friend that I think I want to publish and I'm halfway through it. It is a novel about high finance business deals, but it is really about Chinese spiritual philosophy and a comparison of Eastern and Western economic systems. So far, I like it a lot, and I want to finish it in the next few days. The weather looks beautiful, sunny and warm, maybe too warm, but I'll see when I go out.

As I cross 6th street and approach the park entrance, I am suddenly certain that one of those women with the flower suitcase will be there today. This is another thing that happens to me all the time. I just know things and when I know them with this certainty, they always turn out to be the case. I was excited and uneasy at the prospect of seeing one of those ladies again. But if she was there, and she would be, I was definitely going to talk with her. I entered the park and started walking toward the fountain in the center where I usually sit. There she was. It was the first lady, the one in the white pantsuit. As I got closer, I could see how attractive she was. Her hair was pulled back tight. Her skin was a beautiful olive brown. She looked Hispanic or Middle Eastern, it was hard to tell. She had beautiful eyes, big round and brown. As I approached to sit on the bench near hers, she looked up.

"Oh, it's you again. I wondered when you'd be back,"

she said with a wide smile that revealed bright sparkling teeth.

"How'd you know I'd be back?" I asked, trying to seem only mildly intrigued.

"Let's just say I sometimes know things, and I am not usually wrong."

"What else do you know?" I asked.

"I know our app showed up on your phone recently." When I heard this, my heart stopped for a second. Holy shit, this was getting real. When my heart restarted it was beating at 10 times its normal rate. The hole in my chest came alive and I felt it opening wide. "Now, I see I've got your attention," she said. And she was looking right at the hole that I felt in my chest, as if she could see it, but I didn't even see it. It was just a feeling. "It's a beauty," she said while nodding toward my chest as if wanting to confirm that she could in fact see it. "We've been watching you for a long time. Since you were very young in fact. Oh, yeah, I know something else important about you. You've been talking to Innocence in your dreams. She's really worried about us, but she's innocent, she worries about everything."

I suddenly felt protective of Innocence. "That's not Innocence, that's anxiety." I said defensively.

"Sorry, yeah you're right. She just doesn't know. Anyway, it doesn't matter. Aren't you going to ask me about the app? I am sure that's what she wants you to do."

"Who are you? I don't even know your name, and you seem to know all about me."

"Oh, sorry, my name is Trust," she said flashing another big smile.

"You women have weird names."

"They're beautiful names," she corrected. I let that comment pass and asked her to tell me about the app. "Well you already know that it's called e-Ternity, but you haven't been able to get into it yet because we downloaded it onto your phone, but we didn't give you a password yet."

"Yeah, OK. But what does the app do?"

"It opens you up to eternity of course. It accelerates your brain frequency to its full potential and at the same time it harmonizes and stabilizes your mind at that frequency. It is a total enlightenment app." I got a chill up my spine. No wonder Bob came to mind today. "You're thinking about your old friend Bob. The stuff he showed you years ago was crude, but yes, we did get the idea from him. It was a brilliant idea, but he was never going to be able to bring it to completion."

"You know Bob?" I asked.

"Not personally, but I know of him. We have had contact with him for a while, but I was never in contact with him myself." She shifted in her seat to make more room on the bench. "Here sit down." Then she reached out her hand. "Want some gum?"

"No, thanks. And given the COVID threat I will just sit here a little further away, nothing personal."

"I understand." She said while taking a face mask out of her purse and putting it on. "I forgot I had taken it off," she admitted.

"What's in the suitcase?" I asked pointing to the flower print suitcase that I had suddenly noticed on the ground near her feet. "You all seem to have the same one."

"It is actually the same bag. Whoever goes out takes it. It's full of books." As she said this she leaned over on the bench and unbuckled the latches on the suitcase. She opened it up and sure enough it was filled with small paperback books. The covers looked similar to the app Icon. It was a picture of the starry cosmos and it just had a title and a subtitle:

**e-Ternity**
**Where everyone is everyone else.**
**A companion guidebook to the App**

"Everyone is going to need a copy of this when the app gets downloaded later this month, but when we're all together we will explain it all to you."

"You mean when we find your other two friends?"

"Yes, we need to go meet them near the river. Are you ready for a little walk?"

# CHAPTER NINE

Innocence and I had no idea what to do. Neither of us knew where we were and as she explained to me, we didn't even know whose dream this was. I learned that often at night we experience ourselves in other people's dreams. There is a great deal of cross-pollination that occurs in our sleeping hours. It seems that as a species, humans use dream states to communicate between individuals sharing skills and information. In this way, know-how can be brought to where it is needed. Of course, as I listened to Innocence explaining all of this to me, I was very aware that I was hearing all of this from within a dream and from a dream character. Is it possible that you can learn about real life from someone in your dreams? Come to think of it, I guess that happens all the time. Right now, I don't know what the difference is between my waking self and my dream self. I have been a lucid dreamer for years, but this is totally different. I can't put my finger on it, but it is not like anything I have ever experienced before.

As we discuss what to do next, Innocence sits still, and I pace back and forth. Occasionally, I look at her and each time I see how beautiful she is. There is something so soft, warm, and - well - innocent, about her face. Finally, we decided what was obvious all along. We have to try to find the plane. Through the trees we can still occasionally see the smoke rising from the wreck. Neither of us has much hope that the plane has anything of value to offer us, but it is literally the only thing we know about. Our choices boil down to just sitting here, walking aimlessly through the woods, or trying to follow the trail of smoke to the plane. And, of course, the plane could have something to offer us. This dream appears to have started when I jumped out of the plane. Neither of us has any memory of getting into the plane and taking off. Neither of us remembers where we were going or where we were coming from. The dreams started in a plane that was faltering. I jumped out, she parachuted down to meet me, and now we are here. That is all we know.

"Ok then, we hunt down the plane," I said, and she nodded.

"Are you getting hungry?" she asks.

"Yeah, a little." And just as I say that I notice something behind a nearby tree. It looks like a box and it is pretty obviously in view, so I wonder how I could have missed it earlier. As I approach the box, I see that it is not a box but a picnic basket. Inside there are some wonderful fruits and vegetables. There are sandwiches, hummus, and cucumber it looks like, and two big bottles of water. "Look at this!" I shout and she runs over.

She inspects the food and says, "Well, whoever's dream this is, they don't want us to starve."

"You mean the dreamer put this here for us?"

"Seems to me. I asked you if you were hungry, you said yes, and boom here it is. I think it is interesting that it appeared to you and not to me. You seem to be more central to this dream than me."

"Are you sure the food is safe?" I asked nervously. She

reached in, picked up a sandwich and took a big bite out of it.

"Yep, it seems fine to me," she said. "Whoever is dreaming this could have killed us with a lightning bolt or blew us up in that plane. Doesn't seem to be any reason for them to go to all of the bother of creating lunch just to poison us with it." Hearing all that I picked up a sandwich and ate. It was all a dream anyway.

"You realize that I only half believe in you?" I confided.

"Come on, you only twenty percent believe in me, if that. I think that will change as things continue though."

"I half…" interrupting myself I correct, "maybe eighty percent expecting to wake up any second and write all this down in my dream diary. I will sit up in bed and I will think, 'Wow, I spent all that time with her.' Then it will be over until next time. I will be back in the real world."

"You will be back in DreamOne, but this is as much the real world as that is. In fact, if when you're there, you think of this as unreal, then this is more real than that. The space between dreams is more real than the dreams themselves. The space where we can see the different dreams that we travel through and recognize that they are all real, is more real than any single dream no matter how real it feels when you are in it." She took the last bite of her sandwich and said, "Let's get moving."

"Should I put the rest of this stuff in my pack?" I asked gesturing toward the rest of the food.

"You can if you want to. I am pretty sure we will find food and drink every time we want some, but yeah, you can carry that."

Once the food and water are in my pack, I sling it over

my shoulder, and we start walking in the direction where we can still see the smoke from the wreck rising into the air between the trees.

After walking a half hour or so in silence, I start a conversation. "I first started dreaming of you about six years ago."

"I've already said that you started a lot longer ago than that; but yes, you started to remember them about six years ago."

I ignored the comment and pressed on, "The first time, I was sitting on the edge of a slow flowing river. It was about a couple of hundred feet wide and I saw you on the other side. I just watched you and you took off your clothes and started splashing water on yourself. You were so beautiful." This last sentence came out with more feeling than I had intended, and I looked over at her nervously. She looked back at me with her big beautiful eyes and smiled. I relaxed and continued. "I wanted to call out to you, to say hello and swim across and meet you, but I was stuck. I couldn't move my lips or my arms or my legs. I could only sit there and watch. Then a bird flew overhead. It was a hawk and it circled in big arcs across the blue sky. I saw you look up and then you quickly scrambled to put your clothes back on before running into the trees and out of sight. I woke up stunned. I couldn't really understand why. It was such a simple dream. It didn't seem to have any particular significance, but I was left with a powerful sense that something very important had just happened." Innocence was walking a few feet ahead of me now and it was a few minutes before she spoke again.

"We are soon going to see just how important that

dream was. I remember that dream. I remember the river and the hawk. I don't remember you. That was the hawk's dream and I didn't like the feeling I was getting from it. If I had noticed you, it might not have seemed so menacing." She paused for a moment and turned back toward me with a compassionate look in her eyes. "I realize it is hard for you to understand all this and it must feel cryptic and unnecessarily vague, but I really have no idea how to explain it all to you."

"I've surrendered to this," I said making a big sweeping motion with my arms to indicate that I meant everything. "So you don't have to worry. It is a dream, and dreams don't always make sense, although they usually feel like they do inside them. Whatever. I'm just going with it. I don't really have any other choice. This isn't the weirdest thing that's ever happened to me. Besides, I want to find out how it all ends up."

"Perfect. That is the perfect attitude to take. You are going to make this a lot easier with that attitude."

The ground started to slope upward and soon we were both slightly out of breath. We stopped talking and walked for another few hours mostly in silence. It started to get dark when we suddenly saw an old rundown cabin ahead. It was just one room with a ladder leading up to a loft. There was a fireplace with a fire lit in it and a large stack of cut wood outside.

"This is exactly the cabin I was just picturing in my mind," I said.

She looked over at me with a mischievous smile. "Next time how about a hotel?"

I smiled back. We were both happy to have a place to crash.

"You seem to be the charm in this dream." she said as she sat on the rocking chair by the fire.

...

I am surprised the old man hasn't felt me out here in this lake. He went inside the dojo an hour ago. What's he doing in there? The water feels nice, but my feet are getting stiff from being so still. There is not a ripple on the surface. Suddenly the screeching sound of a small plane engine can be heard in the sky. Looking through the top of my head, I can see the plane falling downward with a trailing plume of smoke rising up behind it. The screeching gets louder and louder. The pitch of the sound gets sharper. Finally, *CRASH*, the plane hits the ground a hundred yards or so from the old man's dojo. The impact was big enough to make the ground shake and the water quake. That should wake the old man up. They'll all be arriving soon now.

# CHAPTER TEN

I ended up living with Bob and Clarisse for about two years. There's plenty of story to tell there, but it will have to wait for another time. There's way too much story to tell in any one place anyway. During the two years that I lived with Bob we built a strong local community in Boston. We became friends and I got closer to Dr. Free.

I eventually moved to Vermont where Dr. Free's main community had also moved. We lived outside of Burlington, only thirty minutes from the Canadian border. We had a campus up in the mountains with a big main house and seven other buildings. I ended up living there for eighteen years. There were about 85 of us living on the property together and Dr. Free lived there in one side of a duplex. By the end of my tenure, I was living on the other side of Dr. Free's house.

When I joined the community, it was only about six years old, but it was still a bit of a struggle to gain true acceptance. Everyone is extraordinarily open and welcoming, but at the same time there always seems to be a curtain hiding something behind the scene. I just kept at it. I was so happy to be in a place where spiritual freedom and enlightenment were foremost in everyone's consciousness. Day to day life was a dream. We woke up and exercised and then did two hours of meditation. We ate meals together and worked together. At night we had meetings. We would discuss Dr. Free's teachings, community business, or any personal issues that came up. It was all fascinating to me. I had never experienced anything like it.

After I had lived in the community for eight years, Dr. Free called a meeting with his male students. There were about forty of us living there at the time. We all sat on cushions on the floor arranged around Dr. Free's chair. After a few minutes of silence, Dr. Free started the meeting.

"Look you guys, we've been at this for fourteen years and I don't think we are any closer to the goal than we ever were. I know you all love me, and you love this work, but that's not enough. Something big is supposed to happen. You are all supposed to enter into a higher stage of consciousness together. We are supposed to make a collective leap into an awakened life together. And I don't think any of you cares much about it. You're all just happy to live here. You get your three square meals a day and do your practice and then you just want me to back off. Well, I am here to tell you that I'm not backing off. I am going to start pouring it on. I am going to push you all until you either wake up or leave. I don't care if you all leave. I'd rather start all over again with a whole new crew than just limp along for fourteen more years. Do you get what I'm saying?" He paused and there was no response. "Do you get what I'm saying?" he said again much louder.

A number of the older guys responded with enthusiastic agreement. "You're totally right, Dr. Free. We're all way too complacent about this," someone said. I think it was Chris.

"For Christ's sake!" Dr. Free yelled. "Don't pretend to know what I'm talking about. If you knew what I was talking about we wouldn't need this meeting. Just realize that you have no idea what I'm pushing you for. Be humble. All I need to know is that you are with me. I need to know that I can push you as hard as I know I'm going to need to, and that you will respond and make it all worthwhile. That's all I need to know."

This statement was followed by a loud chorus of, "Yes. We're with you."

Dr. Free sat still for a few minutes after the room went quiet. Then he said. "Good, that's all I needed to know." And he stood up and walked out.

One day, word came to us from Dr. Free through his assistant Lori that we would all be doing an additional hour of meditation each day. Then after a week, we were told that we should add to that a mala practice. We were each given a mala which is a beaded necklace with 108 beads on it. We were instructed to say 10 malas, 1080 repetitions, of a particular chant every day. The chant went like this: "My heart is open to the mystery of life. I recognize the higher power in the universe. My life is devoted to expressing that power. I am the cosmos personified. I am That." It takes about two and half hours to complete 10 malas. That meant that with our two hours of meditation and one hour working out, we were now doing five hours of practice each day. It was a lot to get in everyday, especially since our workload didn't decrease, but hell, spiritual practice was what we lived for.

Two weeks later Dr. Free wanted to meet with us again. We all crowded onto the floor of his small living room. He sat on the couch. He had a white board on the wall. "I know you have all been doing the extra practice, but you have to understand that just chanting a few thousand words isn't going to do the work for you. But I am going to give you the benefit of the doubt. Maybe, in spite of the fact that I have explained it you a thousand times, you still don't get it. Maybe you still don't understand why we're doing this, or how it works. I don't know how you couldn't, because I talk about it all the time, but, like I said, I am going to give you the benefit of the doubt one more time and explain it all again." He had been looking at all of us while he spoke, but now he turned to the white board and drew a big circle. "We are going to do so much spiritual practice that we rip a hole in the fabric of space and time. Then each of you will learn to stand like a rock of faith and humility at the edges of the hole." He drew many dots all around the hole. "The strength of your practice will keep you planted. That will keep the hole open and the rest of humanity will be able to pass through it into a new life in a new universe. Do you understand how important this is?" His question came out mixed with a good deal of anger. "We have to do this! You have to do this! You are what I've got to work with. I know you all think you are giving a lot to this, but believe me, you haven't even gotten started."

Dr. Free closed his eyes and sat perfectly still. I felt my mind expand. It felt like gravity was shifting and I was feeling lighter. My consciousness was so peaceful. The vision of human souls passing through to a higher universe had calmed me. I was certain that we could do this. I knew that we could open the cosmos up. I could feel the strength and the commitment of everyone in the room. We were still forty people then. We were resolute that night.

Suddenly, Dr. Free's eyes opened wide. "Good. That's it. Stay with that," he said and then he got up and walked out of the room. We all sat for at least 20 or 30 minutes more. Then one by one we got up and slowly and silently left the room and walked away into the night.

Three days later we got new instructions from Dr. Free. Forget about the malas, they aren't working. Instead, he wanted each of us to do one thousand prostrations every morning. A prostration is a spiritual practice often associated with Buddhism, although they are also done by Christians. You start standing upright, then you lie flat down onto your stomach, and then stand back up again. One thousand of those is a real workout. According to Dr. Free, they were meant to engender humility. The first day we did them it took me nearly three hours to complete the whole one thousand and I could hardly walk the rest of the day.

Eventually, the prostrations stopped, and we started with something else. Then we were told to stop that and something new would be initiated. Weeks went by. We started and stopped nearly a dozen different practices. Finally, Dr. Free asked to meet with us again. This time we were told to meet him in a local bar called the 735 House. Everyone was there a few minutes before the scheduled time of 8pm when Dr. Free walked in. He might have been just a little drunk, but it was hard to tell.

"OK, you guys, the practices aren't working. We need to have a heart to heart. What do you need from me? How can I help? I can't do this for you, but I will do anything I can to help you do it."

I saw my hand shoot up into the air. I couldn't believe that I had done that. I was terrified.

"Tell me, Brian, what do you need?"

"Dr. Free, I don't think I know what we are aiming for.

I don't know what it will look like when 'it' happens. Can you tell us what you are looking for?"

"Brian, I've already told you guys everything I know. I don't know what it is going to look like, but I know that I will recognize it when I see it. And so will you all. There's nothing else to be said about it. You just have to do it now."

No one else raised a hand. We all sat for a long time not saying anything. Eventually, Dr. Free spoke. "Listen, you guys have to figure this out. Maybe getting drunk will help. Here's two thousand bucks. It's all yours. Drink up and talk this out until you know what to do." After saying this, he slapped twenty hundred-dollar bills on the table and walked out of the room. We all drank that night. Some drank way too much. We talked, and we argued, and we talked some more. We didn't really come to anything. Finally, the bartender came into the room and said they were closing. It was 1:00am.

The next morning, we were all pretty hungover and we certainly hadn't any more of a clue as to what we were doing. And we didn't know it, but the pressure tactics were about to increase dramatically.

# CHAPTER ELEVEN

Trust was walking to my right, wheeling the suitcase filled with books behind her on the sidewalk. We had nearly made it to the river now.

"How do you know about Bob and Innocence?" I asked for about the twentieth time. I had been asking questions during our entire 30-minute walk and she had not answered a single one. "Why the fuck won't you answer me?" I said aggressively. I was getting really angry now. She said nothing. Then she bolted across the street and onto the pier. She was getting ahead of me now. She was practically running.

"There they are!" were the first words to come out of her mouth since we were in the park. She seemed authentically thrilled to see them. She was delighted. It was as if they were her best friends in the world and she hadn't seen them in years. If I wasn't so angry about all this, I probably would have found the whole scene delightful myself.

She ran up to one of the other women and practically jumped into her arms. I heard them both squeal. The third woman then wrapped her arms around the other two and they all started squealing. I looked around to see if people were noticing, but there were only a handful of people nearby and they didn't seem to notice at all.

I walked closer and I could start to make out what they were saying. Trust turned to me. "Girls, this is him. This is

Brian. I told you he'd come back."

"He's cute," said one of the two African American women. She was the one I saw on the third day. Her dark blue jumpsuit was fit tightly over her thin, but shapely, body. It had a low-cut neckline that revealed a couple of ribs just above the space between her small but lovely breasts. The faint white pattern I could now see was a series of clouds with little cherubs flying over them. Their wings were outstretched atop their chubby bodies and each had an arrow drawn in a small bow held in its hands. The images were of Cupid, the Roman god of desire, erotic love, and attraction. The son of Venus, the god of love, and Mars, the god of war.

Without any warning the beautiful woman in the dark blue jumpsuit leaned toward the side of my head. I felt her kiss my ear licking it gently with her wet tongue and then biting down smartly on my earlobe before pulling away. "What the fuck," I said softly, but audibly. She looked at me with a huge and magnificently delightful smile. Her white teeth were brilliant and shining. Her big eyes penetrated into my soul. I felt flush, violated, peeved, and sexually turned on all at once.

"Better be careful with her, Brian," said Trust placing her hand on the African American woman's shoulder. "This is Freedom. And believe me she is wild. I don't think you can handle her, so I will watch you two." She winked at Freedom and smiled. Then she looked toward the other of the three women, also African American but with lighter skin tone than Freedom. "This is Surrender. So, now you've met us all. I'm the oldest, Freedom is the baby, and Surrender is in the middle."

Surrender held out her hand. She was wearing a plastic glove and she was also the only one of the three wearing a mask like me. I took her hand tentatively and shook it. "Nice to meet you," she said. Then she offered me some hand sanitizer which I took, rubbing it into my hands vigorously.

"I'm so glad to meet you all," I said looking at these three amazingly attractive women, two in jumpsuits, one in a white pantsuit. "But I really have no idea what is going on. You all seem to know more than me so I would love it if you would explain. Trust said she couldn't explain until we were all together. Well, we're all together." I paused expectantly, but then realized I had something else to say. "And by the way, I am pretty sure this is all a dream. That's why I am just going with everything you say. If this were the real world, I would question a hell of a lot more of this, but since it's a dream, I might as well just sit back and enjoy the show. I'm going to wake up in the real world eventually anyway."

"Of course, it's a dream, silly." Freedom said. "Everything is a dream. What you call the 'real world' is just your first dream. It feels more real just because it was your first. Kinda like the first time you make love. Right?" She winked. "You would all be better off if you realized that your 'real world' was as much a dream as any other. Then you could just go with the flow there, too. Save yourselves a lot of trouble, drama, and trauma."

"Freedom, if we're going to explain all this, let's explain it right. OK?" Trust looked at her and Freedom nodded approval. Trust then looked at me. "If we talk about there being many dreams, and even your first also being a dream, we are giving you the wrong idea. In a sense there are many dreams, but there's only one reality. Reality is the space in which all the dreams co-exist. You see, you are never in just one dream, you are always in the dreamspace. In that space, all the different dreams overlap and intermingle. Any dream character experiences themselves as being in one world, but they never really are. They always exist at an intersection of dreams. Look around," she motioned with her hand to the people around us. I looked. I was feeling a little dizzy.

"You are seeing bits and pieces of at least fifteen or twenty dreams right here. You see that guy over there?" She pointed to an old homeless man talking loudly to himself about a hundred feet away from us. "You should see the world he sees right now." She looks around and points to a beautiful sparrow in the tree next to us. "It's easy to see in his case, but look at that bird, it is as much a part of a completely different world as that old man. That tree, the big one, it figures in at least twelve dreams right now. It's an old one so there is lots of cross over in it. You can think in terms of dreams or you can use the more modern terminology of multi-dimensionality, it all means the same thing in the end. What we call the universe, and what feels like a single universe from the inside, is actually a multiverse of many dimensions that all simultaneously co-exist together. The space within which that multiverse of dimensions exists is the trans-dimensional space of reality. If you are overly identified with your first dream, the one called your DreamOne, then that feels like reality and you will have to integrate any elements that come from any other dreams into your experience of that one. If you can't integrate elements into DreamOne, then you will feel like you are dreaming or hallucinating."

I bent over and picked up a stone. "Is this part of DreamOne?" I asked.

"Yes," she answered.

I picked up a stick. "How about this?" She nodded yes. "How about that river?"

"Everything you can see is part of this dream. They have to be, they are here, but many are also part of other dreams, and you can't see the rest of that dream. There are always multiple dreams crossing over each other. Some part of one dream overlaps and plays a role in another dream. If you think about it for a moment, you know this already. You are here now with us, but you are also with Innocence somewhere. And you are living your past with Dr. Free. That's all happening now, too. Your mind separates everything in time and space, but it is all happening simultaneously right here and now. If you were to open wide enough you would see lots of dimensions of reality all around you."

"I don't believe any of this is real. And you just admitted that it's all a dream. I'm not even going to try to figure any of this out. I'm just going to wait until I wake up and think about it all then."

"That's actually the only thing you can do," said a voice from behind me. "You can't figure any of this out. It is just the way it is. Figuring it out is impossible. You just go with it, like you said."

It was Surrender talking. It was the first time she had offered anything of substance, and I had the distinct feeling that she was someone on my side in all this. She had beautiful caramel colored skin and her one-piece outfit with all of its zagging and overlapping stripes looked like a design from Africa. It was gorgeous and so was she.

"I think he needs a little more time," Trust said reflectively. "Look Brian, we can give you until tomorrow, but you have to be ready by then. So, do what you need to do tonight, and we'll pick you up in the morning. OK?"

"Sure, great?" I said in a friendly voice. It was all a dream, so what did it matter what I said? "I'll see you in the morning. I'm sure you know where I live."

"Of course, we do, sweetie," Freedom said with another wink.

I watched them walk down the pier toward the street. As they reached the street a limousine slowed to a halt in front of them. They all got in and the car drove off.

# CHAPTER TWELVE

During the walk home I thought about how strange it was that I was still asleep. This was the longest most drawn out dream I had ever had. Now I was dreaming that I was walking home along the river. I was dreaming every step. How boring. I walked up to a curb and sat down. How do you get out of a dream this boring? I tried biting my tongue. Nothing. I never remember being lucid in a dream and not being able to wake up. Usually it's the other way around. I have to work hard not to wake up. As I sat there on the curb, a little bird landed on the ground in front of me and looked up.

"Hi there," I said. "I wish I had something to feed you, but I don't."

"I'm not looking for food." I was startled to hear the bird answer back. Now I knew this was a dream.

"What do you want then?" I asked innocently, as if talking to a small bird was an everyday occurrence.

"Innocence sent me with a message."

"Oh yeah, what did she say?"

"She said don't come back. It's a trap."

"What's a trap?" I asked. "What are you talking about?"

"Look, I don't know more than what she said. Don't come back. It's a trap." And with that the bird lifted its head, spread its wings and flew off.

"Fucking great," I thought to myself, or maybe I actually said it out loud. "Now my dreams are messaging me in other dreams."

I got up and continued the walk home expecting to wake up at any moment.

I was in the middle of dinner when the phone rang. I picked up the receiver.

"Hey, buddy. It's Bob."

"Hey Bob, it's been a long time. You still with Dr. Free?"

"On and off, same as I always was. So, tell me, anything weird go on with you the last couple of days?"

"Yeah, as a matter of fact a hell of a lot. To tell you the truth, and I guess there is no reason not to, I am pretty sure this is a dream and you're just made of unconscious memory stuff." Then I told Bob about the three women I had seen in the park and how that had led to my dreaming of meeting them on the pier and all the shit they had told me about multiple-dimensional dreaming.

"Look buddy, I got bad news for ya. You ain't dreamin'. This shit is real."

'What are you talking about?"

"Remember when you wore my bilateral headphones and it knocked your socks off?"

"Yeah."

"Remember that after that I told you I got scared so I dumped that research."

"Yeah."

"Well, I lied. I just moved it to Dr. Free's place. I kept on working on it, on and off, for years. That shit that happened to you made me even more certain that we had something really big going on and Free agreed."

"So?"

"Last week I pulled it out again. I had brought it all back with me to Cambridge, but I hadn't looked at it for a couple of years. I'd been trying to find a way to get more juice out of it at that time, but I gave up. It wasn't working. Anyway, I pulled it out again and I reviewed my notes and I found an obvious error in my calculations. I am honestly not sure how I didn't see it before. Anyway, I recalculated and tweaked the headphones. I turned them on, and the energy spiked so high it blew a fuse. I mean it fried that fuse, melted the wire down to nothing."

"Did you fix it?" I asked excitedly. This was reminding me of old times with Bob. Always hot on the trail of something.

"Yeah, and I told Dr. Free and he said he was coming. He told me to fix them because he wanted to wear them like that."

"You didn't let him, did you?"

"You can't stop Free. At least I never seem to be able to. So, he arrived last night, and we put the headphones on him this morning. He had me wire up the fuse box so it wouldn't blow. Then we put it on him and turned it on. The power went way up. I was afraid it was going to take out the neighborhood. Free had this delighted look on his face. Big smile. Then suddenly nothing. He went completely catatonic. I mean he's breathing and everything. His eyes are open, but he just isn't responding to anything. I was hoping he would snap out of it, but he hasn't yet. I decided I'd give it some time and then I'd call you. I didn't know who else to call."

"You should take him to a hospital. Call an ambulance or something."

"Yeah, of course, I was about to do that a couple of hours ago. I picked up the phone and started to dial. But as I was dialing, Free suddenly woke up and said, 'Stop that! Don't call the hospital. This is important. What the fuck. You initiated this, you gotta let the process run its course or you'll kill me.' So I stopped, and he stopped talking. He went back to catatonic. I'm not sure what to do now."

"Well, I sure as hell don't know what to do. Can you reverse the polarity in the headphones or something and…"

"Oh, shit he's getting up!" Bob said. "Brian, he's up and he's walking out the door. I gotta follow 'em. I'm on my landline so I'm going to hang up, I will call later on my cell."

The phone clicked off. I had no idea what was going on. This was the weirdest dream. Then suddenly I had an idea. I would just go to sleep. If I go to sleep in this dream, I'll wake up in reality. That was the best plan I could come up with. I went to my bedroom and laid down but falling asleep proved more difficult than I had imagined. I lay awake for a long time, until a few hours later the phone rang.

"Hello?" I asked.

"Brian, it's Bob. Look I just got a minute. I'm in the restroom at a diner. Free woke up and wanted coffee. He seems normal. He isn't saying much about what happened to him. He just keeps saying that something big is about to go down and he has to be there. He doesn't seem to know what it is, or where it's happening, but he insists he has to be there when it does. I didn't want him to know I was calling you. I don't know why, just a feeling. But I wanted you to know what was happening. I will call you again when I can. I gotta run now."

"OK, thanks…" I was going to ask him where they were going next, but he hung up.

# CHAPTER THIRTEEN

Free's campaign of pressure had been going on for about four months with tactics that ratcheted up in intensity every few weeks or so. Most recently he had tried sleep deprivation. By then there were only about twenty-five of us left because periodically someone would split. They'd just get up and run off in the middle of the night. You'd wake up and find all their stuff was gone. I'd thought about it myself a couple of times. So, by the time Free started with his sleep deprivation campaign there were only about twenty-five of us left.

Every night Free would have people knock on our doors. You'd be asleep and then you'd hear a loud knocking on your bedroom door. "Wake up, wake up!" someone would scream. "Time is wasting. What are you doing sleeping? Do something! Wake up, wake up!"

Someone would come with the same message about every two or three hours. This went on for two weeks. We lost three more guys during the next three weeks. Who can blame them really? We were all starting to go nuts from lack of sleep.

During this time, we had a group exorcism. A group of women in the community, about twenty of them, met with us in one of the living rooms of the houses. They started speaking to the demon that they said was in us. Shouting loudly. Asking it to leave. Demanding that it leave. The room was getting very intense with shouting. Some of the men started to join in. Then suddenly I saw it. It was a dark cloud of smoke. It rose up over the heads of everyone in the room. It seemed to have a face of sorts. As it flew, we all moved in unison to not be hit by it. We were all seeing the same thing. With one final collective shout we banished it from the room, and it flew up through the ceiling. We all fell into silence. After an hour or more the women started leaving the room one by one. The men sat for another hour and then we each left one by one. It was over. We had battled the demon and won. Or so I thought.

I never really thought it was over. I knew it wasn't because I was hoping so hard that it was. If it was over, I would not have needed to hope because it would have been clear. After a few days I started to have the ominous feeling that something else was about to happen. And then one morning, of the twenty-two of the men that were left each got an invite to a party that was to be held that very night. We all showed up at the address at the appointed time of 10:00pm. When we went in there were about twenty women inside dressed very seductively. They wore so much makeup on their faces that it was almost hard to tell what they looked like. And it was clear that most of them were pretty drunk.

"Come in," invited one young blond woman as I walked into the house. "Here, have a drink." She handed me a shot glass full of whiskey. "Drink up boys," she said now looking around the room. "There's nothing to worry about. No reason to be uptight about anything, life's a party." Suddenly someone turned the music up and the women all started dancing seductively. They would sometimes grab one of us and pull us onto the dancefloor. We all tried to stand around and be unnoticed. It went on for hours this way, until suddenly it all stopped. There we were, just the guys and a room full of empty booze bottles. We cleaned up the mess in silence.

This kind of "dharma theater" as I have since heard spiritual tactics like this called, went on for about eight months. I couldn't possibly recount everything that happened because it was just too overwhelming. There was a dharma theater room set up in which movies played 24 hours a day 7 days a week. All the movies were chosen because they illuminated the blight that Dr. Free felt he was in with us. We were all interviewed on camera under bright lights, like an interrogation of the New Age inquisition and those films were also playing continuously in the dharma theater room. There were times when small groups of people would follow each one of us around and chant to remind us of the urgency of the situation. It went on and on and on. The pressure was immense and generated a sense of desperation in which our responses became increasingly extreme.

Hearing all this it is natural for you to wonder why the hell I stayed involved. I realize it sounds pretty awful, and it was. To be honest, later on when I acted as Dr. Free's personal assistant for a decade, it became increasingly less clear to me how much of his antics were genuine crazy wisdom genius, as it is sometimes known, and how much was misdirected and reckless impulsivity. Despite my later doubts, you have to realize that at the time of all this dharma theater I was a true believer. Every following intervention, as wild and inscrutable as it might be, I took to be a message. I knew that Dr. Free didn't always know what he was doing, but I believed that his hand was being guided by an awakened wisdom that was beyond his own comprehension. If he seemed rash and reckless that was because he was acting on behalf of an intelligence that he himself did not understand.

Even as a true believer, I would experience times when I just couldn't take anymore. At these times I would turn my attention to Rochelle. I would often remember the last time I saw her. It was the day we were to finalize our divorce in the Cambridge courthouse. By then I had been living with Bob for a few months and I had only seen Rochelle a handful of times. So, Rochelle and I decided to meet for breakfast. If you were to have seen us sitting in the restaurant booth with our coffee and pancakes, you might have thought we were on a first date. We were talking about our time together. We were laughing and appreciating each other. It was so strange. Here we were on our way to our divorce proceedings and having an absolutely wonderful time together. I felt everything I had ever felt for her then, and I could see in her eyes and her smile that she was feeling the same about me. "Am I crazy?" I wondered to myself. I have a wonderful wife and I am leaving her to join a spiritual community.

We left the restaurant and arrived at the courthouse. There were five other couples also getting divorced that day. Everyone sat in pairs but not with their soon-to-be ex-spouses. Each spouse sat separately with their lawyer. The judge called each couple up to the stand to finalize the divorce. When she called the names out it was fun to see which pairs got up and walked to the bench. Rochelle and

I sat together, as a couple. We didn't have a lawyer. When our names were called, we walked up together. The judge already had our papers and she called me close to tell me something. "You know, you are entitled to get a lot more than this."

"I know," I said. "But this is what's fair."

"Ok, if that's how you want it. Your divorce is final. Just sign here."

Rochelle was getting the house and just about everything else we owned, but the fact is that the down payment for the house came from her inheritance, so I felt by rights it was hers. I had paid half the mortgage for the past few years, but that was like paying rent. The furniture we had bought together, but what was I going to do with it. And, I was the cause of this split up, so I felt like I wanted her to be set up as well as possible.

This was often the memory that I would return to when I felt like I couldn't go on, but I didn't dredge it up to convince myself to leave. I used it to strengthen my resolve to stay. You see I would think about Rochelle and I would make myself remember that she had also paid a high price for me to be able to live this spiritual life. When continuing on for the sake of my own awakening wasn't enough to keep me going, I would think of her and I would know that I had to do it for her. I didn't want all of the heartbreak I had caused to be for nothing. Rochelle deserved more than that.

I realize that still, any reasonable person would wonder, why? Why did I stay? Why did I still believe? The difficulty in explaining this is why I am so shy about talking about any of this with too many people. You have to pin a great deal of the blame on the strength of my initial experience with Dr. Free. After that night in the yoga studio when I realized that every possible way to live is equally risky, something happened. My head exploded and my chest opened up. For six months I felt like I had spiritual x-ray vision. I could see people's thoughts and I could watch those thoughts start as energy in people's stomachs and then move up into their throats to become words in their mouths. I knew what everyone was feeling around me. I could see the past, present, and future of things. I could vaguely know what was going to happen tomorrow. I could see the energetic flows that had led to exactly what was happening today.

I lived in a constant state of wonder and amazement. I had woken up from the dream of the familiar. I was now living in the reality of the miraculous. People wanted to speak with me. They sought out my advice on everything. Some thought I had magical powers. One guy even wanted me to invest in the stock market for him, I refused. And I was happy in a way that I had never known was possible before. When the experience started to fade, Dr. Free told me not to worry. That was just a taste of what was to come. And over the next few years I had more experiences and each one confirmed the supremacy of the life I was living. Yes, there were hard times, and crazy antics, but there were also beautiful times and I was experiencing a depth of love and intimacy with the people around me that felt like the antidote to all the world's problems. Yes, we pushed each other, we were often harsh with each other, but we also loved each other and supported each other. None of us knew what we were doing and yet we were all willing to try together. In a bizarre way it was very beautiful.

Still, you might not understand, but you have to see that given what I had experienced, the kind of normal life that I saw around me looked crazy. I didn't see many people who were happy at all, and no one seemed to have experienced the deep existential joy that I had, in fact a lot of people wouldn't even believe me when I told them that I had. I saw people going to jobs every day because they had to "earn a living." Many people really detested what they did 40 hours a week and complained about it vehemently, but they didn't quit. So, you could ask me how I could have stayed in this spiritual community so long, but in the same way you could ask almost anyone how they could stay in a conventional life for so long. I suppose the simplest answer to both questions is that sometimes we just don't see a better option. I suspect that lots of people end up stuck in lives they would rather not be in largely because they didn't know there was another option. Perhaps the biggest gift that Dr. Free had given me, at least in relationship to conventional life, was the understanding that there was another option. There was a choice. Once I saw it, I took it. And I didn't want to go back.

So, as I continue on with this story please don't judge me too harshly. If you can try to see it from where I was standing, I think it will all make more sense. They say that hindsight is 20/20, which means that as time passes, we get clearer about things that happened in the past. This does seem to be true, but I suspect it is true in part because we remember less and less of what made it all so complex at the time.

Even during these months of intense pressure and dharma theatrics I was having breakthrough experiences regularly. Once we were having yet another of our dozens upon dozens of all-night meetings. We were arguing over what we were not doing, and what we needed to do. The dynamics were always the same. A few people would have very strong opinions, often opposing, and would be arguing for their positions passionately. The dialog would get increasingly heated. There were always about half of the people who had no interest in participating and sat quietly. Eventually the conversation would turn to the fact that the lack of participation from half the group was the real problem and that would be addressed passionately. One night in the middle of this, I saw very clearly that we were not really having a discussion, we were simply acting out an energetic pattern that we were all stuck in together. I could see the energy swirling around everyone. It swooped and swished around the room. It passed through one person and then the next. It changed color as it moved.

What I saw was that we were not individual entities enacting separate wills. We were all part of the expression of a dynamic energetic pattern that was swirling through us. I started to open up again, the way I had when I first met Dr. Free. The hole in my chest appeared again. I could see the energy more clearly. I could see how it would find each next person, then swoop into them through the base of their spine and travel up the spine emerging with words through their mouth. We were all speaking what that energy wanted us to say. We were captivated by it without realizing it. I started calling this energy out between us. I was speaking with such clarity and confidence that everyone listened. The energy started to shift. We were getting excited. We were seeing reality. We were finding our way out of the confusion. For three or four days I was open and clear this way. Dr. Free asked to meet with me. He encouraged me to address everything I saw. He said this was our breakthrough. It didn't last. After a few days, I started to doubt what I was feeling. I lost the energetic vision. The hole in my chest closed up. I was back in the soup with everyone else. And the campaign continued on.

The mock party brought the campaign of dharma theater to a climax. It felt like a breaking point and in fact we did lose a few people after that night. A few more late-night escapes were enacted and although I was choosing to stay, I could not blame anyone for leaving. For the next few weeks there were no more big interventions, in fact we heard very little from Dr. Free at all. We just went about our daily life and waited for the next hammer to fall. Or for this whole ordeal to come to an end. Then one night, quite late, we got a message that there was going to be a meeting to figure out what to do next. We arrived at one of the big meeting rooms and waited. We assumed that Dr. Free would be arriving to meet with us, but it was Susan, Dr. Free's new assistant, who eventually arrived. "Dr. Free sent a message for all of you," she said officiously. "He says none of you are doing anything. It isn't going to work this way. He said you should all leave right now and not come back. He said don't go back to your rooms. Don't go get anything. Just walk out this door and never come back." With that, she abruptly turned and left the room.

We all stood there, mouths gaping. Dr. Free had just asked us to leave the community. To leave the property that was our home. I was the youngest in the group, and I had been in the community for eight years at that time. The others had all been there longer than that. After a few minutes we all did as we were instructed, as we always did. We walked out the front door and left. We decided to meet at a local diner which was the only thing that would be open at midnight. There were twenty-two men in the group, and we pulled a group of tables around and ordered coffee and then we did what men do: we got practical. We started calling local motels and hotels until we found one that was cheap and could accommodate all of us. We had five cars between us, and we drove to the hotel and moved in. None of us had a change of clothes and only about half of us had our wallets. I am not sure what the lady at the front desk thought as we, a large group of men, entered the hotel well after midnight and rented eight rooms for twenty-two people. I am sure it was one of the most bizarre things she had ever seen, but what she didn't know was that it was going to get even more bizarre.

# CHAPTER FOURTEEN

Beeeep! Beeeep!

The sound of a loud horn outside my house woke me up. I got up from the bed in just my underwear and leaned out the window. It was bright outside and hot. I slept on the second floor and when I looked down, I saw the long black roof of a stretch-limo. And standing just outside of it was Freedom. She was looking up at me and even from this distance I could see her sparkling white teeth not to mention some amazing cleavage which I am sure she was aware of.

"Hi darling!" She said waving up at me. "We're here! Come on baby, it's time to go."

What the fuck? Where is the dream? Wasn't I supposed to have woken up by now? Was Bob's story about Dr. Free going catatonic part of the dream, too? What about the talking bird? Was I still dreaming? Maybe I had just dreamed that I went to sleep, and then I woke up again still in the dream. Or maybe this was all real. I just couldn't tell anymore. It all felt like a dream, but it all felt like reality, too. I tried to run through the sequence of events in my head, but I couldn't get any of it straight. Everything that had happened over the past few weeks was all jumbled up in my mind. I couldn't tell what was real and what might not be. It was all equally real, or all equally not. "It's a trap." That's what Innocence had said. "Don't come back. It's a trap." Maybe I had already come back. Maybe I was in the trap right now. Maybe it was too late to listen to her.

"Don't just stare off into space. Get dressed and get down here. Don't make me have to come up there and get you." Freedom hesitated for a moment and then added, "On second thought, please make me come up there and get you." She winked with an exaggerated movement of her cheek.

"Look it's going to take a minute, I gotta hop in the shower," I said before pulling my head in the window and heading to the bathroom.

A few minutes later I was leaving the front door and heading toward the limo. Freedom was still outside the car leaning against it. She was wearing a short black skirt, flat shoes and a strapless top that showed her stomach. She leapt up as I approached and opened the limo door with an exaggerated bow.

"Welcome back," she said as I slipped into the car. She climbed in behind me and I sat in the seat opposite the three of them. I was facing backwards and could see through the back window beyond the three lovely faces that were looking at me. Behind me was a dark window that separated us from the driver. I could only see his silhouette, but I was sure he was a man and I wondered who it was that was driving these ladies around. I had been thinking in the shower about how I was going to approach this encounter. I still didn't know what was going on, but I was pretty sure this wasn't a dream, at least not an ordinary one. These weren't ordinary women either. They were some kind of spiritual beings, avatars or something. They had an air of superiority that I assume manifestations of supernatural beings would have. They appeared to have direct knowledge of higher realms, and because of that, they treat physical beings with contempt. I had met a few of these higher manifestations in my dreams before and most of them had a similar attitude. They aren't bad beings; they just can't help but feel superior. I guess I can't blame them. These women clearly seem to know a little something about me, but I've kept my cards pretty close to my chest until now, and they haven't revealed that they know too much. So, I'm going to let this play out a little bit and then see if I can surprise them.

They all sat looking at me with legs crossed. They certainly were beautiful women. The small suitcase was also in the car with us. "Ok, where are we going?" I asked.

Trust spoke now, "Our employer would like to see you, so we are going to meet with him. It is a few hours away, but we have plenty to talk about, so I hope you don't mind. After all you don't even think this is real, or have you changed your mind about that?" She paused for a moment and looked at me carefully. "Yes, I can see that you have changed your mind. Do you finally believe we are real?"

"I never doubted that you were real, but now I also believe that this is not a dream."

"So, what do you think we are?" asked Freedom giggling for no apparent reason.

"You are avatars, or some kind of physical manifestation of divine principles. I believe that you are exactly what your names suggest. You are Trust, Surrender, and Freedom. You are those spiritual qualities given a physical form. And Innocence whom I met in my dreams, is another one like you."

The three women looked at each other and nodded in

agreement. They appeared to be impressed with me. I bet they haven't met someone who recognized them and was so comfortable with the truth of who they were.

"So, you see all that, and you are not afraid?" This time it was Surrender who spoke. "In your culture beings like us are not believed to exist. There must be more to you than we were led to believe if you can so easily accommodate us into your reality. Now I am wondering who you are?"

"Yes, please, Brian. Tell us who you are?" Trust said suspiciously.

"Do tell." said Freedom. "We're dying to know."

"Not here," I said and then closed my eyes. I thought I should take advantage of this moment and reveal myself while I had them off balance for maximum effect. I started to relax. The women went quiet. My breathing started to slow. I let the contents of my mind pass by without looking. I started to float in the inner world of consciousness in the way I had learned to do during all those years with Dr. Free. I just let myself get very quiet. My breathing slowed until it was almost imperceptible. I felt so relaxed. I wasn't aware of my physical surroundings anymore. If the car was moving, I couldn't feel it; if there was external noise it didn't exist for me. In fact, I had no idea what, if anything, was going on around my physical body. My attention was completely focused on the experience of consciousness. This will take time. It always does, but they said we had a long car ride so it will not matter that it takes time. And the three of them are curious now and they want to know what I can do.

The meditation is fluctuating. Initially I feel myself sinking deeply very fast, then I start bobbing up and down at the surface of consciousness. I let the fluctuations continue without being bothered by them. That is always the secret. If you want to sink deeply into your innermost depths, you simply have to be content with everything that happens. In the end it will all yield as long as you don't allow anything to distract you. And so, I rest. Rest and relax. Waiting without impatience. Content to sit quietly in the back of this limo with these three avatar women forever. If nothing happens, I will be fine. I need nothing more than this. Relaxation and a growing sense of blissful joy. Being alive feels so good as soon as you forget about everything else.

The slight rumble of the car rolling across the pavement started to feel like the gentle rocking of an ocean. The three women were slipping further and further away from me, or more accurately I was slipping away from them. My breathing was so slow now that my chest complained with a searing pain. It was telling me, loudly, that my body required more oxygen. I relaxed. I allowed myself to feel comfortable even in the face of suffocation. My body, feeling its need for oxygen began to panic. It was demanding that I gulp for air. It desperately wanted a huge inhale. It shivered slightly. I relaxed and finally in one beautiful transitional moment of release my body breathed for me. My lungs filled to capacity and then exhaled their contents. They did it again. The breathing was steady and deep, but it wasn't my breathing. It was the body. To me it felt like I was on a mechanical respirator that was filling my lungs and then emptying them for me. The panic had subsided. My body was now completely asleep. It was stiff, as if dead, all of my consciousness had been removed from it. It was being breathed by the universe now. And I was free.

Those first moments of freedom are the most wonderful experience you can ever have. You feel as if you have peeled away from the body that had felt like it was you. You are floating just above and behind it. I had learned and practiced this ability working with Dr. Free. I had told him about it on several occasions. I was excited to share my discovery of this capacity, but I had soon found that the conversation was unwelcome. I began to realize that Dr. Free had had this experience, of course I knew that because he and I had shared the experience the first time when we had voyaged together, but it seemed that he had not mastered the ability to move into his astral body at will. He was jealous. Our relationship deteriorated after those conversations, but it would still be nearly a decade before we would part ways completely. Again, that is a story for another time.

I began to grow. I rose up above the roof of the car, beyond the treetops. I went all the way out. And then I came back. I shrank back down as I had learned to do. Almost all the way back down, but not quite. I am hovering over my head. The experience of astral projection is delightful and delicate. It is a complete disorientation followed by a reorientation in another form. It is exactly the process we all go through unconsciously each evening as we fall asleep. It is also the same journey that we are all destined to take for the last time at the moment of physical death. It takes a few minutes to reorient yourself once you are outside of the body. I looked down at myself and saw my body sitting cross legged on the wide seat of the limo. I looked perfectly serene and at peace, and of course I was. Slowly I looked over and beyond my head and saw the three women seated opposite my body. Trust, Surrender, and Freedom all look-ing expectantly at my unmoving body.

"Hello there," I called out from my floating position overhead. All three of them looked in the direction of my floating vantagepoint. They stared at me quizzically as their eyes adjusted to my new non-form. Slowly I could tell by the looks in their eyes that they were all now seeing me, or at least seeing a projection of me from their own minds. I could see that they were impressed, even a little apprehen-sive. They were each beginning to realize that they had not been told the whole truth about me. And knowing that they did not know the whole truth about me, meant that I could be anything or anyone. They were all a little worried about what they had stepped into the middle of.

"What the fuck?" I heard Freedom think to her sisters.

"Shut up, Free," thought Surrender in return. "He can hear us thinking now." The tone of Surrender's voice betrayed the fact that she was in fact the leader of this threesome. In embodied form, she played the quiet sub-missive sister, but clearly in reality she was the leader. They must have been thinking to each other constantly while we were together. During all of those long silences they were in constant dialog.

"That's right. I can hear you thinking just fine now. I feel a little more comfortable out here with all of you."

"So, who are you?" Trust thought.

"I see I've got your attention now." I said commanding-ly. "Now, I'm really glad we have a long car ride because we have a lot to talk about. Shall we get started?"

# CHAPTER FIFTEEN

The first three nights at the hotel weren't any different for us. We met in one of the rooms that we had rented and argued about whose fault it was and how we were going to get Dr. Free to invite us back into the community. This was always Dr. Free's ultimate power. Even by that early time in my career with him, I had seen him wield it like a knife many times. The one thing he could truly control was who was in, and who was out. We all wanted to be in, so this gave him a great deal of power. I had seen him kick many people out of the community and then wait until they made some gesture to him that convinced him to let them return. I had never seen him kick this many people out at once before.

It was an awkward three days. Every time I walked past the front desk, I would cheerfully say hello to whoever was working there. Usually it was Johnny, he was the son of the owner, or Sandy, the main front desk person. They were both dead curious to know what was going on, but Johnny would never ask about it. Sandy and I talked a few times and she would gently inquire, "Are you guys doing some kind of work project together?" "Are you attending a conference?" Those kinds of questions. I told her that we were part of a start-up company and we were staying in town for a brain-storming week around a new project. That ended the questions.

Sometime late on the third afternoon I happened to be passing by the front desk when a large delivery truck pulled up to the front door. The driver of the truck jumped out and walked in. As he approached the desk, he asked Sandy, "I have a delivery of flowers for 'The men.' Do you know who 'The men' might be?" He was sarcastic and a bit aggressive with her which made me want to rush to her defense.

"I think I am one of those men," I said assertively. "What do you have for us."

"OK, at least I found you. They're flowers. I'll be right back." He walked quickly out the door and returned with two small vases of flowers and a card in his teeth. He motioned with his head for me to take the card. I was so apprehensive about what I would find in that card that I just took it, and it didn't even occur to me how unsanitary that was.

"To my valiant men, Long live the Revolution! - Dr. Free" is all it said.

"Where do you want this?" the driver asked.

"I can take them," I said holding out my hands.

He handed the two vases to me. "You better get some help if there are more of you. This is a big delivery."

I put the two vases in my room and came back with three more guys. After about 30 minutes we were done unloading. Dr. Free had sent 200 vases of flowers. As he left the hotel the driver looked at me with a mixture of pity and disdain. By then Sandy had now been joined by two maids and they were talking among themselves nervously.

Our meeting that night was particularly intense. Dr. Free's message was clear. He wanted to up the pressure to force us into the same state of urgency that he was feeling about ending this stalemate. There were more opinions, accusations, and plenty of blame to go around. Jacob from Denmark left that night. In the middle of our meeting mayhem, he stood up and spoke in his heavy accent saying, "This is crazy. I'm not going to take any more of this shit!" With that he walked out the door. Yoseph from Israel and Donny from California got up and walked out silently following Jacob out the door. I never saw any of them again.

We ended our meeting, inconclusively as always, at about 3 am. I went for a walk. It was a warm and beautiful night. So interesting how, even when your own life is in complete turmoil, the world just goes on being beautiful without you. As I strode down each suburban street past all the single-family houses, I wished that I lived in any one of them. I imagined what my life with Rochelle might have been. We might have lived in a lovely neighborhood with a few kids of our own. I might have a career and a great salary. Maybe we would travel the world during our vacations. But that is not the life I had chosen, and in my heart of hearts, it was not the life I would want. As crazy as my life was right now, it was the only one I would ever want. I had given everything that I had to the pursuit of awakened consciousness and spiritual freedom. I didn't want anything else. I didn't care what it would take.

The next morning, I woke up abruptly to a hard knock on my door. "Get up!" someone shouted as they knocked and ran past the door. "We've got another delivery." I jumped up, put on some clothes and hurried to the front door. I saw the same delivery man from the day before. We unloaded another shipment of 200 small vases full of flowers. We got another card with another message. "I wonder how many flowers it will take?" was all that it said. The delivery man looked a little spooked. He was probably wondering if he should report all this to the police.

We filled a second one of our hotel rooms with the new load of flowers and then sat together to meet. As always, we start with thirty minutes of silence. Then the endless debate continued. There were still 19 of us left at this point, and the pressure after the second delivery of flowers couldn't be higher. After about an hour of circular arguments, momentary bursts of inspiration, and rounds of accusations, Carl Henderson stood up. Carl had been around in the community just a little longer than me, but he was closer to Dr. Free and generally respected by everyone.

"We've been at this for almost eight months. We're never going to get anywhere this way. Look, Dr. Free just wants us to commit more deeply to our own awakening. He's demanding that we give more of our spiritual heart to this. This isn't a puzzle that we're going to figure out. It's a stand that we each have to take. I am sick to death of these horrible meetings that never go anywhere. Dr. Free just wants us to come back and commit. I'm going to his house and I am going to tell him that I am ready to give all of my heart and soul to this. If anyone wants to come with me, you're welcome to." His words were met with a few minutes of total silence and utter stillness. No one motioned any agreement or disagreement. The truth was none of us knew what Dr. Free was looking for and we were all afraid of guessing wrong. After a few minutes, Carl walked out of the room and down the hall and out of the hotel. He didn't have a car. So evidently, he was planning to walk the half hour to Dr. Free's house.

Carl never came back to the hotel.

The next day we all wondered what had happened. Had Carl been embraced back into the community. Had he been banished even further away. The truth was that just before all of the dharma theater tactics had started, Dr. Free had sent Carl and two other guys to live with his group in Australia. They were helping to 'run the center' we had in Sydney. They were there for three months and returned just before all the dharma theater got started.

Of course, none of us knew what had happened after Carl left the hotel. There were about five of us sitting in the park later in the morning. We weren't talking about much, just wondering if more flowers would arrive. Edward from England finally said that he was going to go see Dr. Free, too. He was either going to get kicked out for good, or he would be accepted back, but anything was better than living in limbo. He left. Evidently, he was going to walk to Dr. Free's house, too.

No flowers came that day. Over the next week nine more guys decided to go see Dr. Free, and seven others decided to call it quits and leave. In the end it was just me and Tommy left. Everyone else had either split or went to see Dr. Free. We never heard back from any of them, either way, so we had no idea what had happened to them.

"You should go see Dr. Free," Tommy said.

"You should, too." I responded.

"I will, but you go first. I think if you go, then I'll be able to follow. As long as there is even one guy left out here, I will never find the courage to do it. In a way, I need you to go back to motivate me to do it too. I want to go back, but I'm afraid to, but I think I am more afraid to be the last one left. Look, you go today and tomorrow, I promise I'll come, too. What do you think? Can you do that for me?"

Somehow Tommy's plea was just enough to get me over my own internal struggle, and I did it. I walked away and a half hour later I was arriving at Dr. Free's house. There was no one around. I imagined that Dr. Free was inside because he almost always was, but there was no sign of anyone around. Of course, I had no idea what to do. I mustered up all the courage I could and went up the stairs to the door. I knocked and after a few minutes there was no answer. I knocked again louder and waited a few more minutes. Nothing. I gave one tremendous round of rapping at the door. Still nothing. I had no idea what to do. Then, out of desperation, I walked down the stairs and onto the lawn. I just knelt down facing the house and waited. I waited for what must have been an hour and nothing happened. I was determined to wait all night if I had to. I was not going to give up.

After about two hours, I heard a car pull up on the street. Three men got out of the car. They were three guys I recognized but didn't know very well. They weren't part of our little hotel group; they were all guys who lived in other countries. Dr. Free must have asked them to come and help out with things while so many of us were away. They walked straight over to me and stood all around me. They were all pretty big guys, so it was definitely menacing.

"You need to come with us," one of them said. I recognized him as another guy from England, his name was Bruce. I had spent time with him when I was there for a month a few years before. He was a great guy. I immediately felt relieved that it was him.

"Sure." I got up and walked with them to the car and climbed into the back seat.

We drove about a mile away and turned down a dirt road that I knew belonged to a local farm. We went a quarter mile or so down that road and pulled over. No one said a word the whole way. We got out of the car. It was hot and I could see mosquitoes flying all around. I was sweating, partly from the heat and partly from nerves. I walked with them into an open field. Once we were about three hundred yards from the car, they stopped.

They positioned themselves symmetrically around me. Bruce stood in front of me and said, "Dr. Free knows you're weak, and you're a coward. If you can't learn to fight you will never find enlightenment. This is your last chance to prove that you can fight."

He pushed me hard, and as I fell backward, I got pushed again, forward this time. I knew exactly what was going on. It was more dharma theater. I needed to fight and fight hard to prove myself. I had seen Dr. Free orchestrate lots of scenarios like this. In fact, during my very first week after moving in with Bob, he and I had done something like this to someone at Dr. Free's insistence.

I pushed Bruce hard to the ground and then I spun around and grabbed the guy nearest me. I think I recognized him as Tim. I decided that I was going to pin all of them to the ground. I released all of my fury. All of the anger and pain of the past few months, the past few years, came down on those three guys. I could see by the looks on their faces that they hadn't expected this level of engagement. Soon I was screaming at the top of my lungs,

"I can fight! I can fight! I can fight for this!"

For the next ten minutes I had the upper hand over all three of them. It was mainly by virtue of surprise, but still I was winning. I somehow managed to get all of them in my arms and they were about to fall over with me on top of them. I might actually do it. I might pin all three of them down.

At that pivotal moment, Bruce wriggled free. He fell to the ground and grabbed me around the knees. I went down hard. Bruce was holding my legs and Tim was laying across my chest holding my arms down with all of his considerable weight. The third guy wasn't someone I knew, and he was a lot younger than Bruce and Tim. I heard a steady sound of thud, thud, thud and with each thud I felt a stiff blow to my right thigh. Thud, thud, thud! It really hurt. I was still struggling to get up and I was still screaming, "I will fight! I will fight!" Thud, thud, thud! I remember thinking, "I'm sure even Dr. Free wouldn't tell this guy to beat the shit out of my leg." Thud, thud, thud!

Finally, I was done. There was just no energy left in me. I slowed to a stop. The thudding stopped. The three guys stood up. I was breathing heavy, lying flat on my back in the tall grass. They walked away and I just lay there breathing very hard, unable to catch my breath. After about ten minutes I heard a call in the distance. It was Bruce.

"Hey, you OK?"

I sat up to look over the grass. I saw Bruce standing near the car. I waved my hand and shouted back. "Yeah! I'm good."

I laid back down and I heard the car drive off. I must have laid there for another half hour before I felt like I could breathe normally again. I eventually got up and walked toward the road. I was trying to decide what I should do next. I started to think that I would walk back to the hotel, take a hot shower, get a good night sleep and go back to Dr. Free's house in the morning. I was limping pretty badly from the pounding my leg took. I had been wearing white pants, which turned out to be a very bad choice. They were covered in green grass stains. Every time I put weight on my right leg, I would feel the pain on my thigh. I pulled down my pants and found a five-inch round purple bruise where all the thudding had happened. No wonder I could hardly walk.

I turned left on the road and started walking toward the hotel. And then I stopped. If I went back to the hotel it would all be over. I would never come back in the morning. And if I did, Dr. Free would never accept me back. I would have proved myself to be a coward. I turned around and walked back in the direction of Dr. Free's house. It took a long time to walk there because I was limping so badly. When I arrived, I went back to the same spot where I had been kneeling before the guys had come for me. I kneeled down and waited.

After only 10 minutes Bruce came out of Dr. Free's house and walked over to me. He sat on the bench near me and spoke.

"Dr. Free says you made it by the skin of your teeth. He doesn't know why, but he wants you here. You are never going to make it unless you learn to fight that hard all the time for this. He says that you should go right now straight to the meditation hall and you should wait there until you hear more."

I shook my head yes and started to get up, but Bruce spoke again.

"Dr. Free says you can leave anytime you want to, but if you do leave, you are never to come back, and you are never to contact anyone in this community again. Do you understand?"

"Yes," I said.

"Then go to the meditation hall."

The meditation hall was just a short walk away. When I walked in the front door, I saw all of the 11 other guys that had left the hotel to talk to Dr. Free. They were all here. Everyone had staked out a little spot for themselves on the floor. It looked like they all must have been living here for a while. I wonder if they all had to fight like I did to get in. I imagined that they hadn't because they all looked shocked as they saw me limp in, covered in grass stains and with long strands of dry hay all through my hair. I wondered how long we would be living here. I wondered what would happen next. I wondered how Tommy was doing. I didn't know it yet, but Tommy was never going to come back.

# CHAPTER SIXTEEN

"I want to know who you work for and I want to know all about that app. What is e-Ternity?" I asked clearly and definitively. The three women looked back and forth at each other. Clearly, for the moment, the balance of power had shifted and suddenly their avatar superiority was nowhere to be seen. I knew that wouldn't last forever, but for now I had the upper hand. "I've had as much as I am going to take. One of you needs to start talking, or thinking, and I don't care which."

Each of the three women glanced at each other again, and without saying or thinking anything, they each took out their phones. They each hit a few buttons on their screens and then Surrender turned her phone toward me. On the screen I could see the small e-Ternity icon in the top right corner and the rest of the screen showed only a field of stars, like you might see on a clear summer's night, or maybe it was a photo taken through a telescope. She turned the phone around now and stared into it. All three of them were staring into their phone screens. Their eyes glazed over and they looked calm and peaceful. I saw their astral bodies begin to separate from the physical. They each expanded rapidly until I could not see them.

I waited for them to return.

After a few minutes I saw their energy condensing again. Now they were each floating above their own heads as I was.

"Now you know what e-Ternity does," said Surrender, "but you can do this without the app. I suppose that is why the app showed up on your phone without a password. In the past it had always come with a password. Each of us got a password in an email when the app appeared for us. You didn't get one, and we pretended it was because we hadn't sent it, but the fact is we don't know what your password is. And now I see that you don't need one anyway. I had wondered about that. The mystery is solved."

"Who do you work for?" I asked. "Who created this app and what do they intend to do with it?"

"We work for Rolland Richards. He's a Zen Roshi and he developed this app. We are going to see him now. He was very interested to meet you," this time it was Trust who spoke.

"Why?" I demanded. "Why does he want to meet me? Is it because I don't need the app to do this? Is that it?"

"He didn't say. He just wanted us to bring you to him. He said it was important, in fact required, that you came of your own free will. We had to find a way to capture your attention and then win you over so you would let us take you here." Trust said and then Freedom added, "No forcing," with a giggle.

I thought I was going to get more out of these women, but I was beginning to wonder if they didn't know anything else. "How did you get hooked up with this Roshi?" I asked.

"We tend to be involved with a lot of spiritual teacher types," Surrender offered in response. "They invoke Trust and me in their students. They almost all want obedience and we can help with that. They tend to be more careful with Freedom. She's great as a lure. She tantalizes people and she is promised to them if they embrace Trust and me first."

"Of course, once they let us in," Trust says glancing at Surrender, "there is no need to actually include Freedom, so generally they never get her."

"'Roshi Rick,' that's what we call him, had been working with us for decades. Then he started to work on the e-Ternity app. He needed to create algorithms out of each of us for the app. We need to serve the same purpose in the app that we had served with his students in life. It took a few years. We talked to him and he learned more and more about each of us. He worked hard, but he kept saying that we were not programmable. He said we simply could not be reduced to code. He couldn't get us into the app."

Freedom picked up from Surrender at this point. "You see we're not…" She paused and looked downward demurely, "DreamOne human. We're human qualities, capacities, potentials. So, I guess we can't be directly programmed into an app because we aren't of this world."

"That's when Roshi had a breakthrough." Surrender picked up the conversation again. Trust was just listening at this point. "He realized that he couldn't program us directly into the app because we weren't of this world. We aren't technically here, but, he realized, our affects are real, and they are here. He stopped studying us and started studying our effects on people. He studied change in skin temperature, brain activity, and any other physiological effects we had on people. He also interviewed people in our presence. He asked them to explain how they felt and what they thought while under our influence. These were tangible effects. These things could be reduced to code. Trust, Surrender, and Freedom could not be programmed, but our effects could be. That is how we got written into the app. When someone stares into the screen they start responding as if we were there with them. That is what gives them access to the experience of e-Ternity."

"How many people have this app?" I asked.

"Just the three of us and you, as far as I know," answered Surrender.

"What were you doing walking around with all those books in your suitcase?"

"Nothing much yet, but the app is going to be launched next month and the book is the expanded guidebook for using the app. We were showing them to some bookstores and distributors to see who will carry the book. Mainly, we will sell them online of course, but it is good to have them in bookstores, too."

"Why are you three doing this? You're not even, ahh-hh, human." I hesitated to make sure I had not caused any offense. "Do you care about money?"

"We couldn't care less about money. Believe me, any one of us can manifest more money than we could possibly use right now if we wanted to. We don't care about money. We care about eternity. Our entire reason for being, our one and only purpose is to assist people in their quest for the eternal reality. That's all we love. That's why we all love you. You have access to the eternal and we love that. You make our existence complete. You are the fulfillment of our purpose. You…"

"Ok, enough already," I said. "This all still feels like a

dream to me." Anticipating how I thought they were all about to respond, I continued, "And I already know that everything is all a dream anyway, so don't remind me."

Just then the car turned to the left. We started bouncing up and down as we drove down a dirt road into what looked like a forest.

"We're off to see the wizard!" Freedom sang out. "We're almost there. This will be fun."

The three women all returned to their bodies. Their physical eyes, which had been staring unblinking into their phone screens, suddenly moved again. I thought about returning to my body but decided against it. Since the Roshi's interest in me has to do with this capacity that I fought so hard for, I thought I should show up in all my glory.

# CHAPTER SEVENTEEN

My first morning in the meditation hall started with a sponge bath in the bathroom sink. We didn't have a full bathroom here, so that was the best I could do. Of course, I still had to put on my old clothes grass stained from yesterday's ordeal. As I was just finishing up in the bathroom, someone knocked. It was Carl.

"Let's go, Brian. Bob's here with a message from Dr. Free. We're all meeting in the big hall."

I scrambled to finish dressing then walked quickly up the stairs to the big hall where I found everyone sitting on cushions in a semi-circle around Bob. I didn't say hello to Bob, as I normally would, as I took a place in the semi-circle. We all sat for a few minutes and then Bob spoke.

"OK, look around. You're it." Bob said as he passed his gaze past each of the 12 of us sitting in front of him. "Do you get it? You're all that's left. Dr. Free met with nearly sixty of you about eight months ago, and this is what's left. Twelve. But you're what he's got to work with and you're going to have to do this now."

He paused for drama and we all sat in silence.

"Here's what's going to happen. You are all going to have the rest of the day to get your stuff moved into the big house. We emptied it out for you. You will all sleep there together tonight and then tomorrow morning at 4:00 am you're going to start a retreat. Here is the retreat schedule."

Bob gave each of us a piece of paper on which was printed the following.

| | | |
|---|---|---|
| 4:00am | to 5::00am | - chanting |
| 5:00am | to 6:00am | - meditation |
| 6:00am | to 8:00am | - prostrations |
| 8:00am | to 9:00am | - breakfast |
| 9:00am | to Noon | - meditation |
| Noon | to 1:00pm | - lunch |
| 1:00pm | to 5:00pm | - meditation |
| 5:00pm | to 6:00pm | - chanting |
| 6:00pm | to 7:00pm | - dinner |
| 7:00pm | to 8:00pm | - meditation |
| 8:00pm | to 9:00pm | - chanting |

Once we all had a chance to look over the schedule Bob continued. "You are going to start this retreat at 4:00am tomorrow morning and the retreat is going to last as long as it takes. Dr. Free says he doesn't know what is supposed to happen, but he is sure he will recognize it when it does. And you will stay on retreat until it happens. Now, any of you can decide to leave this retreat at any time, no questions asked. Just pack up and go. But remember, if you decide to leave you will never be welcome back and you should not attempt to contact anyone here." He paused briefly then added, "From this moment on you should all remain in complete silence. Is that clear?"

Bob's question was met with unanimous nods and gestures of agreement from all of us. No words were spoken.

"Ok, go make whatever arrangements are necessary and be back in this hall at 4am for chanting. Does anyone have any questions?"

No one did. Bob sat in silence. I knew Bob pretty well from the time we lived together in Boston and I knew he didn't love this role, but he was good at it. Later on, during the decade that I acted as Dr. Free's personal assistant, the role of being the messenger would become my bread and butter. I didn't love it either, but like I already said, I honestly believed that every message I delivered was for the benefit of the awakening of whoever was receiving it. That is, until I didn't believe that anymore, and things unraveled pretty fast for me after that. But at this time, my faith in Dr. Free was still building towards its peak so the first thing I did was call the school that I worked at – I was working as a middle school special needs teacher by this time – and told them that I wouldn't be returning to teach in the fall. Of course, the vice principal whom I had called asked me why. I told her that I was having personal issues. She said she would not be able to hold my position. I told her that I knew that. This was going to be an expensive retreat.

...

All afternoon the twelve of us moved into the big house on the hill. Using only gestures and writing on scraps of paper we managed to sort out who would sleep in which bedrooms. Carl, being the unofficial leader among us, also started a cleaning list and put all of our names on it so we could sign up for chores. By 9 pm I was exhausted and lying down in bed. I was so happy. After all these months of unending pressure the idea of being on a silent retreat sounded like heaven. These months had been so awful and as I lay down that night, I could feel a tiny amount of the inner tension starting to loosen up. It would be too much to say that it was releasing, but at least it was holding on less tightly. All I could think about was how intensely I was going to give myself to this retreat. If Dr. Free was putting us on retreat, I knew it was because he thought it would work. I was not going to do anything but be on retreat and give my mind, body, and soul to each and every practice that I would do.

By the time of the first meditation period at 5:00 am the next morning, I sat down and I just relaxed. For months I had been trying so hard to, "make it happen." Nothing had worked. In fact, all the effort I had made seemed to lead me further and further in the opposite direction. All I was going to do now was follow the simple instructions, sit still, be relaxed, and let everything be as it is. If Dr. Free put us on retreat, it was because he actually wanted us to be on retreat, he wanted us to practice deeply, like we never had before. I wasn't going to do anything else.

The magic started happening on the second day. We were actually sitting outside that day and almost immediately I felt my arm go numb. I realized that usually if that happened I would either move or try to ignore it. Both of those were forms of doing something. Neither of them was letting everything be as it is. This time I just didn't do anything. I remained calm and relaxed and the sense of numbness engulfed me in a cocoon of calm energy. I felt like I was meditating in an electrical field. It was like floating on a cloud of contentment. All day I felt nothing but content and happy and relaxed. That feeling was to be my closest feeling for the rest of the retreat.

The real fireworks started during the third week when

one night I woke up at about midnight after just a couple of hours of sleep with a sharp pain at the base of my spine. I woke up and started rubbing my tailbone. It hurt so badly. I got up from bed and started walking around the room still rubbing my tailbone. The pain wasn't getting any better. It actually felt like I had been hit with a hammer. I tried to imagine how I could have hurt it so badly. I hadn't fallen. I wondered if just sitting all day long for weeks could damage your spine. I felt like crying because the pain was so bad. And finally, out of desperation I just sat on the bed.

As soon as my butt touched the mattress, I felt a small explosion in my tailbone and a column of white-hot light burst up through my head. It roared so loudly I couldn't hear anything else. It was so bright it hurt my eyes. My eyes were open, and I assumed the light was outside of me, so I closed them. But the light wasn't outside, it was rushing up through the inside of my head. It roared upwards sounding like a firehose for about thirty seconds. Then it stopped and the last of the light passed upward into space.

"Fuck!" I said out loud to myself. "I think that was a kundalini awakening. I hadn't really thought those were real."

I lay in bed mostly awake until the alarm went off a few hours later. I didn't know what to think. I felt so warm and light inside. It was different from anything I had experienced before. Subtle but completely lovely. All of my practice that next day had a new depth of ease to it. I stopped worrying about anything, even when my mind was frantically concerned with something it no longer bothered me. I just watched it all happen. None of it seemed to have anything to do with me.

Every day after that was like an adventure. New experiences, new insights. All I did was give myself wholeheartedly to my practice. I didn't worry about anything else. When there were breaks, I just walked around slowly outside and loved myself and the Earth and every creature on it. I felt so much gratitude for being on retreat and all I hoped was that it would go on forever. I didn't want to do anything other than this ever again.

A few weeks after the kundalini awakening, I experienced a second earth-shattering shift in my awareness. I was sitting late at night and I was very tired. I was determined not to fall asleep so I was doing anything I could to stay awake. I couldn't really say that I was meditating. I was just trying to stay awake. I was determined that my head would not nod during this final hour of meditation. The feeling of exhaustion was so unpleasant. My nerves felt as if sharp electrical impulses were shooting through them. My mind was muddy, and I had a pounding headache. My eyes kept burning and watering. I was determined not to nod off. I was going to stay awake. It all got so dramatic. I started fantasizing about standing up and running my head into the wall in front of me, just so I would need to be taken to the hospital and this could end. My mind was not in my control anymore. It was simply generating crazy thoughts.

As I sat in this tormented state, a thought crossed my mind. It said, "You're not really tired." And I realized that it was true. Sure, I was experiencing all of the mental, emotional, and bodily symptoms of being tired, but I was not tired. I was perfectly awake. I realized in that moment that the awareness that was aware of this exhausted body was not itself tired at all. That awareness was just as bright and awake and happy and free as it had ever been. If I were just waking up and looking out at the golden sunshine of a new day, that awareness would not be any more or less awake than it was right now.

Suddenly I didn't feel tired at all. I was amazed. I was experiencing the inside of an exhausted body, but I was not exhausted. I was the awareness that was aware of the exhaustion. I was free. I was happy. I was examining, in the minutest of detail, the experience of being exhausted. It was fascinating to see what it looked like from the outside. Then I realized that I had never been tired, I had never been anything, hungry or thirsty or hurt or even happy. I had always been the awareness that experienced all of those things, but that awareness was just awake, that's it. When I became cognizant that I was the awareness that is aware, an experience of blissful freedom overcame me, but I knew that I was not that either. I was the awareness of the blissful freedom. I was awake and that was all.

As I laid down in bed later that night, I felt like I was floating independent of my experience of being human. I watched my body lay down in bed. I was aware of my body and my personality beginning to relax. And I was aware of insights that were arising as a result of this new experience. I knew that even when I was asleep, I was awake. I knew that I had been this awareness, fully awake, before this body had appeared through my mother's womb. I knew that I would continue to be this awareness that is always awake even after this body ceased to function. I am the awareness that is awake, eternal and free.

As I laid down in bed, I felt my muscles relax and then my toes started to go numb. I just watched as the numbness expanded and engulfed my body just like it did in meditation. Then I was aware that my body had fallen asleep. My breathing was regular and beyond my conscious control. I was being breathed, more than I was breathing. I was asleep, but I was still awake. It was amazing and thrilling. I had just watched my body fall asleep, but I had remained awake. I was the awareness that is aware, and that awareness hadn't gone any place.

My body and my mind relaxed more deeply. The sensation of my body began to disappear until there was nothing left. No sensation of having a body. Nothing at all. Just awareness with nothing to be aware of. I was simply a free-floating consciousness drifting in a space that did not exist. I was the sensation of being that could not be eradicated. I was the eternal and everlasting experience of existence itself. So peaceful, so empty, so free.

Then I was lying flat on my back. But it wasn't me. It felt like me, but it wasn't. I was lying on the ground and my legs and arms were being pulled on very hard, by four huge men. Around those four men was a ring of about ten beautiful young black men. They were all chanting, "You've got to let go. You've got to die." Over and over again.

I was dreaming. I had been nothing and no one floating in no space and no time, and then I was lying flat on my back being pulled apart. It all happened as suddenly as turning on a light switch. I was disembodied and then instantaneously I was embodied. I was dreaming. Or rather, the mind was dreaming. Some neurochemical electrical discharge had flicked it on, and now it was dreaming. This was a space beyond lucid dreaming. I was not dreaming and then realizing that I was in the dream. I was the aware-

ness that was aware of being awake, and was also aware of
being asleep, and then became aware of the dreaming. I was
outside of it all.

The rest of the night passed with dreams coming and
going and in between there was just free-floating awareness
with nothing to be aware of. This was how life was. I was
experiencing what life is. Life is this free-floating. ever-pres-
ent awareness that moves in and out of dreams, in and out
of lifetimes. It is aware of them all, but it isn't any of them.

The next morning at breakfast I sat across from Carl. I
was still experiencing only the awareness that is aware and
nothing else. At one-point Carl and I happened to look
into each other's eyes. We were transfixed. Our mutual
gaze had adhered. I was looking into his eyes and he was
looking into mine. I was aware that I was looking at myself
there. The awareness that was looking through me into his
eyes, was the same awareness that was looking through his
eyes into mine. We were one. I had no doubt. And even
though we never talked about it, I knew that Carl had no
doubt, too. Suddenly I couldn't understand why I couldn't
see through Carl's eyes, or everyone's eyes. They were all my
eyes too, after all. There was no difference. Why did I only
seem to have access from the vantage point of this body? It
didn't make sense anymore. After that I spent many hours
on retreat trying to see through other people's eyes, and
even though I was never able to, I still knew it was possible.
I knew that the only reason I seemed limited to my own
eyes, is because the habit of assuming that I could only
look through my own hadn't been broken yet. I knew that
if I tried hard enough and long enough, I could break that
habit and then I would see all over the world from every

eye there was.

I spent the next three days blissfully beyond and above everything that happened. I was the awareness that was aware and nothing else. At some point I started to worry, and I wondered if this was healthy. But on the fourth night, I fell asleep the old-fashioned way. I laid down in bed, relaxed and then opened my eyes when it was morning. I had come back into my body. Of course, I was disappointed, but I was also determined to be grateful for the experience I had just had, and kept moving forward. This is what I have discovered is most sacred and critically important to spiritual growth. Be grateful for everything you receive and keep moving. Never try to recapture an experience you had before. Never assume that anything has gone wrong. Instead, I always assume that I am given every experience that I need, when I need it, for as long as I need it, perfectly. If it goes away, it could only be because that's what I needed. I have trained myself to be grateful for everything that happens and keep moving.

We did not end up being on that retreat forever, like I was hoping for, but we did stay on for a few more weeks, two months in total, and as miraculous as things had already been, the best was still yet to come.

# CHAPTER EIGHTEEN

The three women walked a few hundred yards on a cleared path through the woods with me floating overhead. Eventually, the trees gave way to a cleared area. There was a beautiful Japanese styled building there and a lake beyond it.

"There's the zendo!" Freedom shouted excitedly.

The structure was exquisite. It was entirely built of wood that was a deep orange and red color. It wasn't painted, but it may have been stained to bring out that particular hue. It was a large square building with a high pointed peak in the middle. From the peak, heavy curved beams descended in great downward sloping arches toward each corner. The beams jutted out a few feet beyond the wall and created an outer roof to cover the porch that seemed to wrap around all sides of the zendo. The walls were wooden with large windows of glass in them.

The orange and red structure sat amongst the trees and looked so natural that you might have thought it grew up from the ground all by itself. We appeared to be approaching the zendo from the front. Behind the building, on both sides, I could see a lake stretching out. I didn't know where we were, but I was sure we were either in upstate New York of the southwestern corner of Massachusetts.

As we walked in the door, we entered a small coat room where we were to leave our shoes. Each of the women took off their shoes, slipped on loafer type slippers that were waiting there in abundance, and then placed the shoes they had walked in with on one of the shoe racks. I, of course, was floating above and behind them, with no tangible shoes to remove. We then slipped past the wall and into the main room. It was beautiful. Wooden on three sides, each graced with a large set of windows, but the wall opposite the door we had walked in was glass from floor to ceiling. Looking out that window you could see a pristine blue lake. The edge of the lake was a few hundred feet from the zendo, and the land had only a few scattered trees on it. Beyond the lake you could only see the continuation of forest with a mixture of deciduous trees and evergreens.

As I looked through the window out over the lake, I thought for a second that I saw someone out there floating in the water, but then it vanished. Just at that moment I heard a door open behind me and to the left. I shifted my gaze and saw an old man walk in through a doorway that I hadn't noticed before. He looked to be in his eighties, maybe older, and yet he walked with strength and physical confidence. He had a long white beard and a bald head. He was wearing a white rope that fell almost to the floor revealing black slippers that covered his feet.

"Hello, I've been expecting you," the old man said. As he looked in my direction, I immediately recognized who it was.

"Is this Roshi Rick?" I asked Surrender.

"Yes, it is," she said.

"Oh no, it's not," I said, then turning back to the Roshi I said, "You're Harry Haralson, right? You were Dr. Free's first teacher. You initiated him in kundalini awakening."

"You must recognize me from the few photos that Free kept lying around even after he stopped working with me. Very perceptive of you, but then again, I would expect that you would recognize me. I am your spiritual grandfather after all."

"Yes, I recognize you from some picture I saw years ago."

"I see that you have decided to come disrobed of your body in your astral form. I would join you, but at my age it takes too much effort and I must conserve what strength I have left. I trust that my associates here," he motioned toward the three women who had walked in with me, "have explained things to you, although undoubtedly not to your satisfaction. Is there anything specific you would like to inquire about?"

"Yeah, like everything. I don't feel like I've been given much information at this point. I know you created the e-Ternity app. I know you couldn't program their qualities directly into it and had to settle for programming their effects on people. The app seems to be able to give someone access to e-Ternity, but I think you and I both know it only simulates an experience of e-Ternity. It doesn't give anyone true direct access to it. I'm guessing that you think I have some secret that will help you create e-Ternity 2.0 or something like that. And that's all I know so far. So, anything else you can tell me, I'm all ears."

"Well, I would say you are quite well informed and there is probably very little left to say. I don't think I can explain the technical side of how e-Ternity works. I didn't actually do the technical work you see, and besides I'm pretty sure you wouldn't understand it if I could."

Just then we all heard the front door open. Then there was the sound of shuffling as at least two people took off their shoes and put them on the shoe rack just outside the door.

"Oh, perfect timing," said Harry, "Our last guests have arrived."

The front door opened and in walked Dr. Free and Bob. Dr. Free seemed startled and looked directly at Harry Haralson.

"Hello, Harry. This is a surprise." And then Dr. Free noticed me in the room. "And my old friend Brian. How interesting, feels like a reunion, one I would have skipped if I had known I was invited."

Free only looked at me momentarily and I could see that my floating energetic form bothered him. He had seen me do this a couple of times before and he had never liked it. Initially I thought he was protecting me from becoming prideful and arrogant about this new-found capacity, but I realized eventually that he was jealous. As I believe I've already mentioned, our relationship deteriorated fairly quickly once he found out what I had mastered. I remember the first time I had told him. He was initially very excited about it, but when I explained exactly how it happened, he got angry and said, "So what? Do you think you're enlightened now? Because you're not, and don't forget it." I had not been thinking that I was enlightened. I was just astounded by what was happening. I hadn't even had a thought yet about what it might mean about me. Free and I could hardly talk after that. He once walked into a room where I was and said, "Just seeing you makes me angry." For about a year, I believed that he was seeing something about my unworthiness and he seemed to use every opportunity to reinforce that assumption. After a while I realized that he was jealous and soon after I left.

Harry ignored Free's comment and addressed Bob instead. "Hello Bob, it's nice to see you again, thank you for coming."

Dr. Free looked at Bob with a flare of anger in his eyes. "You knew he was going to be here? Is that why you insisted we come?" he demanded. Bob ignored him and addressed Harry.

"Hi, Harry. We got here as soon as we could." Then Bob looked over in my direction. "Hi, Brian," he said softly and then added, "I'm glad you found your way here." Finally looking at the three women who stood close together under a big window, he said, "Nice to see you all again."

"OK, Harry," I said abruptly. "You asked if I had any particular questions. Well, I do now. What the hell is going on here?"

Before Harry had a chance to answer Dr. Free turned to Bob and shouted, "Give me the fucking headphones!" Bob obediently drew them from his bag and Free put them on. "Turn them on!"

Bob reached into his bag again and I saw him turn a knob on a small metal box. A faint electrical hum could be heard and then I saw Dr. Free move into his astral body. His physical body now standing frozen and seemingly lifeless exactly where it was.

"There. That's better. Maybe you won't ignore me now," Dr. Free said to me. In his light body form, he was hovering above his body and smiling triumphantly. I ignored him and he turned to Bob. "What the hell is going on, Bob?"

"I've been working with Harry for a few years..." Bob

started to say.

"And you didn't think to mention that to me?" Dr. Free interrupted.

"I'd signed a non-disclosure agreement. I couldn't say anything." He paused and went on. "Look, I didn't realize who he was when this got started. He worked through her," he said pointing toward Trust. "She showed up at my house and seemed to know all about an app I had once created called e-Ternity. It was what I was doing before I got into the headphones. I could never make the app work, so I gave up on it. But evidently, Trust here – that's her name by the way – had heard about it, or rather Harry had heard about it and sent Trust to buy the tech from me. I was pretty happy to sell for the price they were offering, but I had to agree to a seven-year contract as a consultant. And during that time, I couldn't say anything. Neither Trust nor Harry have called me for a couple of years, but the contract isn't up until next November. I thought they'd given up on it. Then Brian told me about these three women he had been seeing and I put two and two together and realized they had actually finished the fucking thing. Who would've guessed that? Right?"

Bob now turned to Harry, "So you figured it out. You wanna tell me how it works?"

Harry briefly explained how he had switched from trying to code the qualities of Trust, Surrender, and Freedom to instead coding the tangible effects of Trust, Surrender, and Freedom.

"Yeah, I can see how that would work. But the app still doesn't give real access to eternity. It just simulates access to eternity. It's not much better than these," Bob pointed to the headphones on Dr. Free's head.

"Of course, it's better," said Harry. "First of all, think about delivery. I can deliver an app to any one of billions of people around the world in a heartbeat. Try distributing that hardware all over the world."

Bob nodded in agreement, a rare acknowledgement from the man who is generally the smartest man in the room, well at least in his own mind.

"But that's not the most important difference. The app works fundamentally differently from those." Harry pointed to the headphones. "You have to wear those for them to work. The headphones don't just initiate an experience of eternity, they actually manufacture it. The experience only lasts as long as you wear them. If I pull those things off Free's head, he'll get yanked right back into his body, painfully I bet." He seemed to chuckle quietly to himself as he had this last thought as though he were thinking of trying it just to see what would happen. Dr. Free looked momentarily concerned as if he were bracing for a rapid descent back into the body.

"With the app you just stare into it for a few minutes and it initiates a neurological pattern that becomes self-sustaining. Initially your body has to continually be staring into it, but once you master the state, you can put the app down and turn it off and the experience will continue. It doesn't last indefinitely, but every time you feel like you are coming down, you just look into the app for a minute or two and away you go. The effect can last for hours and in some people days or even a week or two. No headphones required. That is much, much better." Harry crossed his arms and waited for Bob's response.

"Ok, it's better." Bob said seemingly unimpressed. "But it is not essentially different. As I was saying a minute ago, they both simulate an experience of eternity, neither of them gives you actual access to eternity. You and I both hope that simulating the experience might trigger an actual awakening, but we don't have evidence that it will. Neither of these is likely to lead to the next golden age of humanity."

"Yes, I know that. And that's where he comes in." Harry now pointed toward me. "You see him sitting there. Just floating out of his body all by himself. How did he get out there with no support? Right here we have a living prototype of what we want to create. We just need to find a way to code his capacity and put it in the app. That's why I had my three lovely assistants," he looked at the three women with a big smile, "bring him for this little gathering."

Harry then looked at Dr. Free, "And you. You somehow managed to have him right in your community and missed it. You were always so blind by your own desire for power that you couldn't see what was right in front of you. When I heard that you let him slip away... no, worse... drove him away, I could hardly believe how blind you could be."

Dr. Free looked totally bewildered. He seemed to understand that he had somehow been missing something very important and yet he was still having trouble figuring out what it was. I am sure that the fact that it seemed to have something to do with me, a person he had dismissed almost entirely as worthless, made it that much more difficult to grapple with.

"I think you're all missing the point," I said. "Whatever you might be able to code from my experience, it will still not have anything to do with eternity. The awareness that is aware cannot be understood. It cannot be reduced to code. It is what is and only what is. And that is the whole point. The very idea that you would need an app or a set of headphones or anything else to access eternity is a negation of eternity. Eternity isn't something separate from you. Eternity is what you are. You, me, and everyone else is already that. Introducing the idea that there could be a need for technology to connect you with what you already are, becomes an obstacle in itself. Don't you see? It will never work." I was getting very heated up about this. I was speaking louder and louder. I had everyone's attention and just then I heard a muffled scream that seemed to come from behind a small door just to the left of the main door that exited the room.

"Who is that?" I demanded, but before anyone could answer I heard Surrender shout out from behind me.

"Who is *that*?!"

I turned around and saw a small boy walking out of the lake. First his head appeared then his neck and shoulders. When the water was about as high as his waist, I could see that he was only about three or four years old. And he looked very familiar. In fact, I realized with a terrible fright, that I knew exactly who that was.

"Who is that?" Freedom said again louder. "Who is that little boy walking out of the lake?"

"That's me!" I shouted as I rushed past Freedom and through the window in an energetic blur.

# CHAPTER NINETEEN

I was still in the lake with the water up to my eyeballs watching the zendo. I had seen all of them arrive. First, Brian floating above the three sisters. Then a little while later, Dr. Free and Bob. The six of them had been in the zendo long enough now. They were never going to figure anything out without me. They would just argue and debate without enough clarity between them to see the truth. It was time for me to put an end to this foolishness. It was time for me to get out of this lake. So, I started walking slowly out of the water toward the shore and the zendo beyond it.

"Should I come, too?" my mysterious invisible friend said.

"No, not yet. Wait until I call for you. You will know when it's time."

"OK."

# CHAPTER TWENTY

Even after I had returned to sleeping unconsciously at night, the feeling of not being completely attached to my body remained throughout the rest of the retreat. As the days continued to pass, I found it absolutely effortless to meditate. I only got up because the bell rang. I felt as if I would be happy to sit forever. If the bell didn't ring, I don't know what would have gotten me to stop. At the same time, I felt no need to meditate either. I was totally fine meditating or not.

Each day I woke up. I just opened my eyes and I started to get up out of bed without any idea of who I was or where I was. It didn't bother me at all that I didn't know anything, I just woke up and started moving and I would gradually remember that I was on retreat. I would get dressed and I would walk outside and toward the meditation hall.

I wasn't engaging with thoughts. I was just walking. Thoughts were floating passed the mind's eye, but I was not even tempted to look closely enough to see what they were saying. They just floated by like an anomalous cloud in a clear sky. I looked at the trees and the grass and the dirt path ahead of me and it all looked so beautiful. Sometimes I would walk out of our property onto Summer Street so I could walk past the cornfields of the farm next door. I could see the corn grow week by week. It was so beautiful to see that something that just shot up out of the ground was becoming something that could be eaten. One day I spent an hour writing a letter to the farmer explaining how beautiful his farm was and how sacred and holy his work was. I never mailed the letter, but I loved writing it.

One morning I was sitting in meditation with my eyes slightly open. I was looking lazily downward toward the carpet in front of me. I sat cross-legged, and I wasn't doing anything. I was so happy just to sit there staring at the ground. I felt completely relaxed. I didn't need anything. I was simply sitting and breathing and being conscious. I was awake and nothing more. I wanted nothing more than just to be there. It is hard to describe what it is like to want nothing at all, to feel so full and so complete that nothing could possibly add anything. It feels like being finished with life, finished and ready to rest right here forever, not doing anything at all.

As I sat in that state of perfect contentment, which I was beginning to recognize was my true home, my breathing became very slow and then my body fell asleep. Just like it had that first night in bed. My body fell asleep and I stayed awake inside it. It was asleep sitting up. It was being breathed now by the universe. I didn't even have to pay attention to breathing. I could just sit in unbroken peacefulness and rest. My body would just sit and breathe all by itself. This is what meditation had become for me. Just relax and let my body fall asleep and then sit in the recognition that all I am is the awareness that is aware through the body. I could do this forever.

On this particular morning as I was looking down at the carpet in front of me, I noticed that it was slowly getting further and further away from me. I seemed to be moving upward away from the floor. I didn't move a muscle. I just watched the floor slipping further and further away. Then I was high enough that I could see the wall in front of me. Then I was nearly as high as the ceiling, and just when I thought I would bang my head on it, I passed right through it. I saw the cross section of the wood that the ceiling was made out of. Then I was up in the attic and I could see all the dust on the attic floor as my line of sight passed by it.

Then I moved right out through the roof. I saw the trees around me and the lawn of the meditation hall below them. I could see the road and as I moved higher, I could see all of the other buildings on our property. As this happened, I was simply calm and relaxed, just the way I had been meditating sitting on the floor looking down at the carpet. I could still feel my body numb with sleep and breathing rhythmically. Soon I could see the lake at the edge of the property and then the church steeple downtown. Higher and higher I went, until I could see the lights from the highway stretching across the hills below.

It occurred to me that I should be terrified, but I wasn't. Soon I could see over the mountains and I could trace the ridge of the Appalachians as it snaked north and south from me. Eventually, I could see the Atlantic Ocean way out in the distance. I couldn't see the meditation hall anymore or even the lights of our little town. I could still see the lights on the highway, but only faintly and soon they were gone too. Why wasn't I terrified? I should be terrified. I was so high up, I could see the curve of the Earth. I was so mesmerized by all that I could see. It was so beautiful. Now the Earth was just a beautiful blue and green ball below me.

I could see the line of the sun's shadow as it stretched along the surface. For a long time, I just looked at the beautiful sphere of the Earth below me until it was just a tiny dot of light, no different than any of the millions of stars that I now saw all around me. I had no idea which of the tiny white dots was the Earth that I had just left.

I was truly lost in the cosmos. I had no idea where my home planet was. I had no idea how I would get back to it. I should be terrified, but I wasn't. I was perfectly calm. In fact, I felt wonderful. I felt more at home than I ever had. I felt safer than I ever had. What could possibly happen to me out here? What could possibly go wrong? It was just wonderful. Millions upon millions upon trillions of stars all around. It was so beautiful. It was like nothing I had ever seen. And my body was still numb with sleep, perfectly at rest. My mind was calm and clear. I had no memory of where I had just come from or what I was doing. I was absolutely adrift in an infinite sea of stars and I was happy, deeply happy in a way I had never been before.

The sense of expansion slowed down. It gradually came to a complete rest, a dead stop. The journey was over. I was the size of the entire cosmos. I was the entire cosmos. I was home. I felt the most beautiful and tremendous love imaginable. It was a sense of pure caring, pure affectionate splendor. It shined on and through me. I had never been so loved and I felt so much love in the universe. It was loving like I had never known love before. I was being loved and I was loving at the same time. Loving life. Loving beauty. Loving all of creation.

I don't know how long I rested there. I have no idea if there was even any way to know, or any time to measure out there. It could have been an hour or a year or several lifetimes. I have no idea what that would even mean. What I do know is that the experience of loving peaked at an intensity that left me feeling like I couldn't possibly take it for another moment. Then, I started to come back. I descended, or I shrunk. The return was much faster than the ascent had been. The Earth became visible again, and then the oceans. Soon I could see the New England coast, then our lake. I fell through the roof of the meditation hall and there I was again sitting on the floor looking at the lined pattern in the beige carpet. I was back, but this no longer felt like home. It was the farthest possible place from home. Of course, any specific place was the farthest place from home, when home was every place at once.

I sat with tears running down my cheeks. I had never been so happy.

No, that's not true. I suddenly remembered something. I had been exactly this happy, many times when I was a small child. I would run into the bathroom of my parent's house and I would lock the door behind me. I would face the full-length mirror on the back of the bathroom door, and I would stare into my own eyes. I would look through my eyes until I saw who was behind them and then I would grow. I would go up through the roof of the house until I was bigger than the world. I would keep growing until I was as big as the whole universe. I would feel this very same love. I would feel it and I would know that I was home. Then I would shrink back into my small body and leave the bathroom.

My tiny life seemed like a terrible mistake, but at least I knew I could always get home.

Until, that is, I couldn't anymore.

I was no older than four, the day I walked into the bathroom, locked the door behind me, and started to stare into my own eyes. Nothing. I tried so hard. I tried to remember how I had always initiated the expansion before. Nothing. I tried. I panicked. I didn't know what to do. I was lost. I was truly lost in this little tiny world. I didn't know how to get home. My spirits were crushed. I was overwhelmed with grief. How could this have happened? Why had I been abandoned here? How would I survive?

Soon I entirely forgot about my cosmic trips. I was a regular little boy, who fought with his brother and traded baseball cards. But I never felt normal. I always felt like I didn't belong. I had a deep feeling that something was wrong, that I had lost something and needed to find it, but I had no idea what it might be. Something very important had been lost. And I somehow knew that it had been lost in my mind. I knew that all of the thoughts and worries that were always crowding my head were keeping me from seeing something very important. I tried to stop my mind. To see past it. It never worked, and so I got good grades, went to college, succeeded in a good career and married a lovely woman named Rochelle, but you already know all that.

Sitting there staring at the carpet, I still felt perfectly relaxed. Tears were streaming down my cheeks. It all finally made sense. I knew why I was here. I knew why I had dedicated myself so completely to this crazy spiritual life. I had lost something very important as a child and I would do anything to find it again. And I finally had. I had finally found my way home.

# CHAPTER TWENTY-ONE

I hovered five feet above the boy who was now ankle deep in lake water. It was me. Initially, I recognized myself from photos in the family photo album, but now that I was up close I felt the hair standing up on my arms and a chill running through my spine as I realized that I was looking directly at myself.

"Do you know who I am?" I asked.

"Yes, I know you. You're the one who went away and got lost. Why didn't you ever come back?"

"I couldn't remember how. Then I forgot about home all together. But even so I kept trying. I kept trying to get home even when I didn't know what I was doing. I tried. I tried for years. I finally found my way, but I didn't know what to do when I was there."

"You see that's the problem right there." The boy was a bit round. He was wearing pants that were cut just above his knees. They were grey and a bit big for him. He wore black suspenders to hold them up. He had a white short-sleeve button down shirt on. It was buttoned all the way to the top, even on this hot day. He had his pudgy hands in his pockets and a very intense, deep look in his eyes. He wore brown shoes and white socks, but of course, the shoes were soaking wet, as was everything else he was wearing.

"That's the problem," the boy continued, "The idea that you would have to remember how to get home, is the only thing in the way. You are home. You are home now. You couldn't be anywhere else. You were home, and then you were born at home, and you have been home ever since, and you will be at home until you die, and then you will go home. Do you get it? There is no place but home."

"But…" I began bewildered, "When I expand to the edges of the universe I feel the love and I know I am home. I feel like I have returned to the place that I belong. Here," I looked down at the ground below me, "I feel like I am heavy and limited and burdened by life. Can't you see the difference."

"Ok, we have to move faster than this." I could hear the front door opening on the other side of the building and people were starting to come around to find out what was going on. The boy, or rather, I, seemed to have something he/I had to get across before they arrived.

"It's so difficult without her around," he said, and then he looked up at me sternly, "The first thing you have to do is get her back." I had no idea what he was talking about, and he didn't explain, he just continued. "So, I am going to say this as best I can. You are going to trust me and then you are going to do whatever needs to be done." I started to talk but he shook his head to stop me. "No, don't say anything, it will only get in the way."

The three women rounded the corner of the building with Freedom at the front. She ran shouting, "He's so cute! Look at him! So cute!"

The boy took a deep breath and looked at me with his round and penetrating eyes. "You are the dreamer of DreamOne. You are the creator of this world. You can do anything you want, so stop them."

I imagined them all frozen, and lo and behold, they all stopped. The three women all with smiles on their faces captured in mid run. Bob and Dr. Free and Harry were behind. They had been walking briskly, but now they were frozen in time.

"Oh my god, did I do that?" I asked.

"Of course, you're the dreamer here." He continued, "That was good by the way. You listened and just did it without trying to figure out how. Do you see how that is the key to everything? You have to know it is possible. Knowing it is possible is what makes it possible."

"Yes, Dr. Free stopped time that way when I first saw him teach."

"He didn't do that, you did. He helped you believe, albeit unconsciously, that it was possible to stop time, but you did it. You are the dreamer of DreamOne, not him."

The implications of what he was saying were beginning to overwhelm me. I felt dizzy and weak.

"Slow down. Don't try to take it all in at once. You're only human you know." I swear the little boy winked at me when he said that, but he might have just been squinting. After all, he was staring up at me into the sun.

"Here is what you have to understand. You are not special. Everyone is the dreamer of their own DreamOne. Everyone's DreamOne feels like reality to them, and all the DreamOne worlds intersect and overlap. You cross in and out of your DreamOne world into and out of the DreamOne worlds of others all the time. But right now, at this moment, all these people are in your DreamOne world. I wanted all of you here because something has gone wrong and it's starting to affect too many worlds."

"Who are you?" I asked confused.

"I am you."

"Then I wanted them all here, and I wanted you here, too."

"Now you're catching on. This was all your plan. You made up this plan as you arrived into your DreamOne body. There's never enough time to think through the plan as you pass between lifetimes. It all happens so fast; the plans end up all sketchy with big gaping holes in them. It's a wonder that things work out as well as they do." The boy had wandered off into a thought, but now returned sharply. "Anyway, we're – you're – going to fix this little problem. So, get them all started up again, and I will call in the big guy, and you let her free."

I looked down at the little fellow and I was about to ask for clarification when he shouted up at me.

"No! Don't think about it, just do it. Get them started and set her free."

I turned and looked at the six frozen figures and they all started moving. I felt a tug on the back of my spine, and I heard the boy speak. "Ok, Big guy. It's time." I relaxed into the tug behind my back and suddenly I was in the limo with my legs crossed. "You can come out and show yourself now." I heard the boy say as if I was still hovering above him. I opened the limo door and ran into the front door of the building. I didn't think about what I was doing. I just followed whatever my body was doing. I didn't take off my shoes. I ran straight through into the main hall and over to the closet where I had heard a muffled cry. I tried the door. It was locked. I heard more muffled cries. I kicked open the door with one swift snap of my right leg. The door opened with a loud thud.

There she was. The woman with the auburn hair, Innocence. She was tied to a small chair with her arms behind her and a gag tied over her mouth. It took me a minute to do, but I got the gag off of her and started working on the ropes that bound her.

For an instant I felt like I was out hovering over the lake, looking back at everyone on the shore. They were all looking in my direction. "I need another minute," I said. "Give me a minute, the ropes are tight."

I was back, untying the ropes.

"What happened?" I asked Innocence. "How did Harry get a hold of you?"

"You didn't know it, but you led me right to him. He's been looking for me for years, but he needed to get me into DreamOne, so he could imprison me here. We were running through the woods and you blinked out. I knew you went back to DreamOne. I kept running and you kept running silently beside me. When we got to this zendo something strange happened. It was like we walked through an energy barrier and shifted into a new world. I don't understand why, but your dream self being there with me was what made the crossover possible. I shifted into DreamOne and Harry grabbed me."

"Innocence, I just found out that I'm the dreamer of DreamOne, maybe that's why."

"Maybe. Anyway, Harry was obviously expecting you to be embodied because he was quite distressed when your body showed up empty. Did you get that undone yet? If you're the dreamer just imagine them off."

The binds came off.

"You are definitely the dreamer here; you should start taking advantage of it," she said.

We both ran quickly around the building to the lakeside. As I rounded the corner, I saw a being. It was at least 100 feet high. It was a silhouette of a person. It looked very familiar. It was me. The body was filled with stars. The silhouette appeared to be a hole cut into the fabric of reality that opened to a vast universe of stars beyond it.

I stopped. I stood silently. I saw the bathroom mirror in front of my eyes. I saw the pattern of the carpet on the floor in front of me. I started to expand. I was hundreds of feet above the cosmic me. I saw the small boy and the seven adults around him. I saw my still and empty body closer to the zendo. I saw the entire lake. Then I saw the whole globe. I expanded and the love and bliss returned. I was on fire with it. The expansion stopped. I was the size of the entire universe again. I saw my little boy's eyes in the mirror in front of me. I saw the carpet on the floor. I saw my body filled with stars and galaxies full of more stars. The love was so big. I would have cried like a baby if I had had eyes to cry with.

Then I shrank. I saw the lake and the zendo and the adults and the boy. I stopped about 100 feet above the lake water. I looked down at my starry body. It was a tiny, but impressive, replica of my true cosmic being.

On the shore everyone was looking up at me. Dr. Free, Harry, and Bob looked frightened. Trust, Surrender and Freedom looked happy. Innocence looked... well... innocent.

"Look at her," I said pointing my star-filled arm at Innocence. "Do you see what you did? You hid her from the world. In order to make your technologies work you needed people to believe that you knew the answer to the mystery. You needed people to believe that the secret of existence had been figured out and hardwired into a set of headphones or coded into an app. But, without realizing it, you robbed them of their innocence. You took away the one true freedom they had. The freedom to not be certain about life. The freedom to be open to a mystery beyond what they know. Innocence is the key that opens the door. Innocence is the ground for Trust, Surrender, and Freedom, not the other way around. You were trying to give people access to eternity, when what you needed to do was inspire them to innocence. You needed to help them feel safe without knowing. That is where freedom lies. To live in darkness and explore the adventure as it appears in each moment, not in mapping it all out and capturing it in a device."

I was simultaneously in my adult body looking up at the starry cosmic me, and in my little boy body looking up at the starry cosmic me. And I was the 100-foot-high cosmic replica looking down at everyone else, too.

"It is time to make this right," I said from my starry perch above them all. "We need to support innocence in the world again. Take care of people and help them feel safe enough to trust and surrender to life. Not convince them that they need our app. That's when they can truly surrender and trust, and that's how they will discover what true freedom is."

At hearing their names used this way, the three beautiful women looked at each other and then bunched into a group hug. Innocence was standing very still and, it seemed, maybe shivering slightly. Freedom reached over and grabbed her and pulled her into the hug with the other women. Bob stood between Harry and Dr. Free. None of them looked frightened anymore. They were simply listening.

"I don't have more to say. Don't try to figure any of this out. Just open your heart and then do what feels most natural to do. You know what to do, even if you don't realize that you do. Maybe consuming the fruit of the tree of knowledge of good and evil got things started on the wrong foot. The age of reason sealed the deal. From then on, we have distrusted the inherent wisdom of our being and become blind adherents only of what we could figure out with our minds. Some things can't be figured out, they can only be known. They can be acted on if you are willing to act blindly. That is the return to innocence that you can help bring about. If you choose to."

"Let's go back home," I said to my little boy self, and with a great woosh the boy grew in size until he merged with me within the cosmic replica. Then the cosmic replica grew until it was too large to see. It simply faded into the background.

I was back in my DreamOne body again on the ground outside of the zendo, but I still had inner access to both the little boy and the cosmic being of eternity. The three of us had become one again.

Everyone else stood in silence.

# CHAPTER TWENTY-TWO

Dr. Free was the first to speak. "Let's get out of here, Bob. This is ridiculous. These people are crazy and Brian was always a fool."

"I'm not going." Bob said firmly, "I'm gonna stay and see what I can do to help."

Dr. Free stood. Stunned. He had already played his hand. He had shown he had no interest in whatever effort this group might make. "Give me the headphones then," he said, reaching out his hand.

Bob handed the headphones over to him and Dr. Free walked a few steps away and then turned back. "And your car keys." Bob threw him a set of keys and Dr. Free disappeared around the building.

Bob looked at Harry. "I think I have an idea about how a new app could work, one that would help people to relax into innocence."

"I think I know what you're thinking, but it will be tricky, maybe impossible. We'll need your help, too," Harry said looking straight at Innocence. She looked over at me as if asking for my permission.

"You were all just listening to me, right?" I said. "We can't build an app to restore innocence. We have to find a way to make the world safe enough to relax in. We're going to have to think way outside of the box for this. I know we can do it, and I know that you are each here for an important reason."

Trust and Surrender both nodded.

"Of course, we'll help," Surrender said.

"Yes," added Trust.

Freedom jumped up and down in little rapid hops and silently clapped her hands. She was in.

"What about Dr. Free? Won't he cause trouble?" Bob asked, to no one in particular.

"I don't think so. He'll come around, and he'll play his part," I said, but I didn't really believe it. I was afraid that his part might be that of the nemesis, but if it was, it must also be important.

"You know what?" I asked rhetorically, letting the words flow out of my mouth without knowing what I was about to say, "I think we should all go on retreat together for a while. We need to learn how to expand to the edges of the cosmos...without tech. And we need to embrace innocence and cultivate the qualities of trust, surrender, and freedom."

I looked over at Innocence, "You can help us with that. Right?"

Innocence looked up with that captivating look of wonder and calm uncertainty that made her so irresistibly attractive.

"I don't know," she said honestly.

We all laughed with relief. She was helping already.

# Thank You

Thank you for reading this novel. I deeply appreciate the time you take to read my words and I sincerely hope that you find it time well spent. If you are curious about other novels that I have written, please visit **www.transdimensionalfiction.com** and sign up to receive my newsletter.

Made in the USA
Las Vegas, NV
23 July 2022

52071207R00105